"Where did you get this?"

"Someone left the file on my desk for review. The documents inside look like they've been copied, but when I compared it to his report in the database, the file contained extra information."

"But Randy's been dead for more than a year, and the crash was ruled an accident. Why would someone give this to you now?"

"Maybe because I reopened Randy's case."

Skye's eyes widened at his announcement.

"Do you remember what happened after the collision?" Jake asked. "Do you remember seeing anyone there?"

"A few flashes come back to me every now and then. The man tonight at the library had a skull tattoo inked on his arm. I remember the same tattoo from the night we wrecked."

She turned her gaze to his. "When I was under sedation, I dreamed the same man stabbed Randy in the neck with a knife. I figured the dream was my brain's way of coping with the trauma."

Her words confirmed Jake's theory. "I think the dream was your brain's way of uncovering the truth. And now they're coming after you."

Shannon Redmon remembers the first book she checked out from the neighborhood bookmobile, sparking her love of stories. She hopes to immerse readers into a world of faith, hope and love, all from the beautiful scenery of her North Carolina mountain home, where she lives with her amazing husband, two boys and white foo-foo dog named Sophie. Connect with Shannon on Twitter, @shannon_redmon, or visit her online at www.shannonredmon.com.

Books by Shannon Redmon

Love Inspired Suspense

Cave of Secrets
Secrets Left Behind

Visit the Author Profile page at LoveInspired.com.

SECRETS
LEFT BEHIND

SHANNON REDMON

LOVE INSPIRED SUSPENSE
INSPIRATIONAL ROMANCE

LOVE INSPIRED® SUSPENSE
INSPIRATIONAL ROMANCE

ISBN-13: 978-1-335-72316-1

Recycling programs
for this product may
not exist in your area.

Secrets Left Behind

This is a work of fiction. Names, characters, places and incidents are either the product of the author's imagination or are used fictitiously. Any resemblance to actual persons, living or dead, businesses, companies, events or locales is entirely coincidental.

For questions and comments about the quality of this book, please contact us at CustomerService@Harlequin.com.

Love Inspired
22 Adelaide St. West, 41st Floor
Toronto, Ontario M5H 4E3, Canada
www.LoveInspired.com

Printed in U.S.A.

For I know the thoughts that I think toward you, saith the Lord, thoughts of peace, and not of evil, to give you an expected end.

—*Jeremiah* 29:11

To the one man who has encouraged, supported and
loved me through this amazing writing journey.
Trent, you're my light and my life.
i thank Jesus for you, every day.

ONE

Skye Anderson scoured the library shelves for her four-year-old daughter's favorite board book, but *Blue Bunny's Bonkers Birthday* hid from sight. Her fingers combed every spine, touching all the other stories, many of which she'd donated to the annual drive last year on June 16—the day her husband, Randy, died.

The patter of rain on the glass outside triggered memories of his fatal car crash, which she pushed aside, and worked faster on her task at hand. The library would close soon, and the strict attendant at the front would shoo her from the premises if she remained past seven.

She glanced at her watch. Three minutes to go.

"Not it. Not it." Skye tapped each book with her finger, then rounded the last stack near the back hallway, crouched and made a mental note to count all the day's squats into her workout app.

"Please be here."

Near the end of the row, like a beacon in a vast

ocean, a blue rabbit ear curled around the back of the cover. Skye grabbed the book and smiled, remembering all the sweet moments she'd shared, reading this story to Romi, but she wasn't here for reminiscing.

With a quick flip to the back, Skye lifted the flap and found the hidden microchip Randy had discussed in a letter she'd discovered locked in a desk drawer after his death. If only she'd cleaned out his office sooner, then maybe she wouldn't be stuck in the middle of the local library at closing time.

"There you are," she said, wishing Randy was here to ask him all the questions running through her mind right now. She remembered him fiddling with the book while they were at Romi's riding lesson the night of the accident but had paid him little attention.

She tucked the chip back in place and closed the cover when the buzz of the overhead fluorescent lights snapped off.

Silence surrounded her.

Skye, still kneeling on the floor, glanced around. White spots danced in front of her eyes while her vision adjusted. She stood and peeked around the corner. No one sat at the square checkout cubicle located in the middle of the room. The front door was closed, and the librarian had turned off the neon Open sign.

She stood, her boots clacking against the tile

floor, and slipped the book into her oversized crossbody bag for safe keeping. Had she known the important information the chip held, she never would've made the donation.

Randy had instructed her to take the chip to the only officer they trusted, Sergeant Zain Wescott at the sheriff's department, upon his death. Zain's wife, Carli, was her best friend and babysat their daughter.

Something thumped to her right.

Skye paused and listened. Wind and rain pounded the windows, filling the space with the white noise of nature sounds. Shadows of tree branches swayed and clawed against the glass, dispersing the dim glow of the streetlamp outside. Nerves tingled and crawled across her skin as she continued toward the exit. With a pivot, she glanced behind her again. Nothing but darkness.

Skye took a deep breath. No one else was here from what she could tell, but despite the rationale, her heart rate increased and amplified the soundtrack of paranoia playing in her mind.

A movement on her left caught her attention. She quickened her steps and dashed for the door. A large man stepped into the aisle under the Exit sign, bathed in the glow of crimson.

She turned and bolted for the side door. He chased her, jerking strands of her hair, and whipped her body backward. Her head struck against a hard object. She twisted and fell, palms down on the cold tile floor.

Dizziness invaded her vision, and pain dazed any mental acuity remaining. Black boots stepped close. She lifted her gaze. A red skull tattoo scarred his forearm, and a ski mask covered his face. In one swift motion, he hoisted her under his muscular bicep, squeezing her neck. The Exit sign grew smaller as he hauled her back into the center of the room.

"Got her." The man's deep voice echoed off the walls. No accent or distinguishing rasp.

"Bring her here." Another male voice filled the space.

If she didn't fight, then they'd kill her.

Skye dug into her bag still secured across her body, grabbed her pepper spray, aimed, and pressed the ridges on the trigger. The potent con-coction struck her attacker's eyes. He released a curse and his grip, giving Skye enough room to run.

She crawled inside the librarian's cubicle with-out being seen, hid underneath the counter and retrieved her phone from her bag. She placed the device into night mode so the glow from the screen wouldn't divulge her location, then texted 911.

Need help
Crystal Creek Library

Being attacked

An ellipsis emerged, then gave way to a response.

Help is on the way
What's your name?

Skye Anderson

Footsteps plodded toward the desk, and Skye grasped the phone to her chest. There wasn't one attacker, but at least three.

"Find her."

"I saw her run toward the side hallway. I'll check there."

"If you find her, kill her and get the chip. Also, have Hawk activate our contingency plan, in case the cops show."

Skye's body trembled with the man's announcement. She needed to get out of here and make a break for the door. The half wall encircling the librarian's workspace opened on two sides. She waited for footsteps to disperse, then crawled out, keeping hidden in the shadows. She peeked around the corner. The Exit sign glowed red and marked her only way to safety. Skye broke into a run, while praying for God's protection with every step.

* * *

Detective Jake Reed returned to his desk with a strong cup of coffee in his hand. His partner, Nate Steele, leaned back in his seat and stretched.

"Only five hours to go—" Jake took a swig of his caffeine-laden drink, hoping for a jolt of energy to finish out the shift "—until my first week back at the Crystal Creek Sheriff's Department is over."

"You know we have rules to follow—one being that newbies must bring their partners coffee for the first year," Nate replied.

"Nice try. I'm not that gullible."

"Fine. I'll get my own. By the way, I tossed a couple more files on your desk for us to go over."

Jake shuffled through the folders while Nate disappeared into the lounge area. The third file caught his attention. He flipped open the cover, and a photo of his late best friend, Detective Randy Anderson, graced the front.

Jake read through the reports, but this was not the first time he had reviewed the details. Six months after Randy's death, he'd logged into the system from his previous job at the Charlotte precinct and noted a few discrepancies. When he returned to Crystal Creek and took the open detective job months later, he'd asked Sergeant Zain Wescott to reopen his friend's case after presenting his findings. His superior officer agreed.

Jake refreshed his memory with the details—Randy had died in a fatal car wreck, and his death was ruled an accident. All the information about the case was here, including evidence Jake hadn't seen when he logged in to the database before. He flipped to the medical report, where a sticky note marked a line describing the wound on his friend's neck. Something didn't add up.

Nate returned, sipping from his steaming mug.

"Hey, listen to this." Jake swiveled in his chair and rolled closer for his partner to view the contents. "The trauma doctor's description of Randy's fatal neck wound doesn't match the account given by the officer on scene. The officer said a smooth piece of glass made the cut into Randy's neck, but if those edges were smooth, then why did the trauma doctor describe the wound as jagged and torn?"

"Why are you looking into Randy's old accident file?"

"It was in the batch you put on my desk."

"That's strange. Randy's case file has been closed for a couple of months now and I didn't have it pulled."

"Maybe Zain put it on my desk. He agreed to reopen the case. I figured you knew and brought me his file with the others."

"Nope. Didn't know a thing about it." Nate pointed at the two files on top. "Those are the ones I pulled. Maybe Emma made a mistake and mixed in Randy's folder."

"Who's Emma?"

"The assistant out front."

Jake kept reading. "The medical examiner stated Randy died instantly from a severed carotid artery, but their little girl stated her father released her mother's seat belt after the collision. How can a dead man unbuckle a seat belt?"

"What are you saying?"

Jake flipped through a few more pages. "I don't think Randy's death was an accident."

Nate stared at him for a moment. "Of course it was. Our officers checked out the scene along with the medical examiner, Natalie Kensington. We all agreed."

Jake wasn't so sure and continued to peruse the information. Nate's phone vibrated, grabbing his attention. His friend read a message and reached for his blazer on the back of his chair. "We've gotta go."

"What's going on?"

"Patrol's been dispatched to the library. An attack is happening and could turn into a hostage situation."

Jake downed his last sip of coffee, no longer needing the caffeine given the adrenaline pumping through him. "Don't we have a hostage unit?"

"No, Detective Big City. We're a small department and have limited resources."

Jake grabbed his blazer, too, and quickened his steps to catch up with Nate. "Who's the victim?"

"Randy's wife, Skye Anderson."

The name churned Jake into action, and they both sprinted to Nate's SUV, then ignited the sirens and blue lights when they hit the main road. The Crystal Creek Library stood a mile from their downtown building, but with Skye in danger, the trip felt like an eternity. He had to get to her in time and keep the promise he made years ago while in the police academy. His vow to protect his best friend's family upon death superseded any troubled history or years of separation. There was no better officer or friend than Randy and Jake owed the man his life.

Voices yelled after her. Gunshots fired. Skye ducked and wove as she raced for the door. Two more stacks and she'd be there.

A body slammed against her from the left. Skye hit the floor with a thud and slid into a table displaying the latest bestsellers. A tall vase toppled and crashed to the ground, splintering glass shards across the floor.

Pain shot through her spine and seared the nerves into her fingers with a burning sensation. A metallic taste tainted her lips from the gash on her head. She clambered to her knees and grabbed a thick book from the shelf.

Her attacker lunged as Skye swung the object. The momentum connected against the side of his head, knocking him to the floor.

Sirens echoed closer, and the faint hint of blue strobed through the large windows at the front of the building. More gunfire popped around her, and she charged for the door, tumbling into the cooler night air. Sheriff's cars swarmed to the front of the building, screeching to a halt. Officers spewed forth while aiming their weapons on her.

"Hands in the air," they said in unison.

Skye dropped to her knees, raised her hands, and waited, glancing over her shoulder. Her attackers didn't emerge. Probably due to the vast number of cops stationed outside the building. They must have another exit strategy.

Skye dropped her gaze to the sidewalk. She didn't want the officers to consider her a threat.

Brown leather shoes with tassels stepped in front of her. She lifted her gaze—dark gray slacks, navy blazer with a rocker tee underneath. Familiar blue eyes met hers when the man knelt to the ground.

"Jake?"

He grabbed her hands, helped her up, then hurried them both away from the front entrance.

The adrenaline coursing through her body

faded into disbelief at the sight of him. Jake Reed hadn't graced the city limits of Crystal Creek in almost seven years, when he left her heart broken.

Now, the blue lights reflected off his badge and highlighted the word "Detective." The only open position had been Randy's.

He turned and focused on her forehead. "Are you okay?"

"Not really."

"Any idea who would want to hurt you?"

A multitude of thoughts swirled in her mind about the microchip, the scary memories of Randy's death returning and haunting her dreams, as well as a billion questions to explain why Jake left her and never looked back, but now wasn't the time to bombard him with personal inquiries.

Instead, she shook her head without a word. If she was going to keep her daughter safe, losing her senses in front of her former boyfriend and current Crystal Creek detective was out of the question.

She would have to figure out, on her own, why someone wanted the chip Randy left behind and was willing to kill her for the information, before they returned and left her for dead.

TWO

Red lights from the ambulance bounced around the walls of the small parking garage. Jake escorted Skye to the back of the vehicle and helped her inside. He folded down a seat across from the stretcher and out of the way so the paramedic could work.

Her face was pale, and she avoided his gaze. "You took the open detective job?"

"Yeah. I should've called you."

She shrugged. "Not like we've kept in touch over the years. You can take whatever position you want. It's your life."

A life his best friend, Randy Anderson, had saved, protecting Jake from his abusive, alcoholic father. He wasn't sure where he'd be without the man. Maybe dead.

Jake motioned to the paramedic and pointed to the gash on Skye's head. "Can you take a look at her cut? It doesn't want to stop bleeding."

The man lifted a few dark curls and touched

the area around the injury. Skye flinched with the pressure. "It'll be okay in a bit."

"Needs a good cleaning." The paramedic rummaged through drawers inside the cab. "Looks like we're out of betadine swabs. I'll get some from the other unit and be right back."

He left Jake and Skye alone, a palpable silence between them. She fiddled with the edge of the sheet underneath her. "I don't need a medic."

"It's protocol. They'll clean you up a little and your daughter won't have to see blood down the side of your face."

He shifted in his seat and tried to think of something interesting to say. They hadn't been alone in years, much less talked. Jake had ended their relationship seven years ago and moved away to work for the Charlotte Police Department. Skye wanted marriage and a family, and with his abusive upbringing, he wasn't built for that kind of life, but Randy was.

Jake had witnessed, more than once, how his best friend looked at Skye. Most men would've been jealous of a best friend's secret feelings for their girlfriend, but not Jake. If his absence could give the two most important people in his life what they wanted, then the sacrifice was an easy one to make and he left after graduating from the police academy.

He didn't return for their wedding or the birth of their daughter, but Randy still reached out to him throughout the years, keeping in touch and sending him emails. The last correspondence, about a year ago, listed his friend's wishes if something happened to him in the line of duty— the first red flag alerting Jake something was wrong.

Skye touched the cut and pulled back her fingers, tinged with blood. He grabbed a glove and a couple of gauze pads from an open drawer, then moved beside her.

"Let me see if I can help until the paramedic gets back. Can you pull the right side of your hair out of the way?"

She pushed her dark curls over one shoulder and exposed the still-bleeding cut. His fingers brushed through her hair, lightly feeling the full length of the injury. He ignored the honey scent of her shampoo and the long shape of her neck. She was still the most beautiful woman he'd ever seen, but he wasn't here to rekindle an old flame. He'd made his final decision a long time ago.

With pressure applied, he lifted her fingers to take over the task. "Press right here."

Skye placed her hand on top of the gauze. "Thanks."

"No problem. I'm sure he'll be back in a minute." He motioned with a thumb over his shoulder. "Make sure to ask for some ibuprofen, because you'll probably have one nasty headache."

A knock rapped on the metal ambulance door, and Nate stood in the opening. "Our officers did a sweep inside the library. The men who attacked Skye are gone. They had a way out through the back of the building."

Jake removed the glove from his hand and tossed it into a red biohazard bag. "Let's pull the security footage and see if we can get a tag number or description of their vehicles."

"We checked. There were no cameras on the back side, and no one saw them leave. Sergeant wants us back at the office in an hour to brief him."

"Sounds good. I'll be done in a few minutes."

Nate walked away, leaving them alone again.

"I can drive you home. With your head injury, you really shouldn't be behind the wheel."

Skye folded her arms across her chest. "Why arc you here, Jake?"

"You called 911. We were dispatched."

"That's not what I mean. Your life is in Charlotte. You took a detective job with the homicide department there and, from what Randy told me, excelled in every way. Why would you come back and take a small-town detective's job for half the pay?"

He hesitated to tell her the real reason he'd returned, fearful she might not understand or, worse, refuse to cooperate.

"My mom's not been doing well, and I moved back to take care of her."

Her tight expression softened. "I didn't realize she was sick. I hope it's nothing too serious."

"Her diabetes worsened, and her medications got mixed up. The doctor thought having family here to help her would be best."

"Then I guess you're staying for a while?" Her green-eyed gaze met his, and he wondered if she wanted him to stick around.

"For a while."

The paramedic climbed back into the ambulance. "Got the swabs. Let me get you cleaned up, then we can figure out our next steps."

Skye sat up a bit straighter. "My next step is to head home to my daughter."

"We should take you to the hospital for a brain scan, make sure you don't have an internal bleed," the paramedic said, cleaning the wound and wrapping her head with a bandage.

"I'm not really a fan of hospitals. I'll be fine."

Skye stood when the medic finished, and Jake stepped from the ambulance, following her back into the parking garage. She turned and faced him. "Thanks for helping me."

"Where are you parked?"

"My car's way over there, near the front entrance." She pointed and dug in her bag for her keys. "I'm fine. Really. Driving helps me clear my head, and I could use some downtime."

"At least let us follow you home. I want to make sure you don't end up in a ditch somewhere."

"Jake…" She faced him again and exhaled. "No offense, but I don't need a babysitter. I feel fine. Besides, the attackers are gone. Nate said so. I doubt they'll follow me home."

She pivoted on her heel and hit the key fob to her car, parked about a hundred feet away in the open-air section of the lot. Taillights flickered, and a small beep chirped through the air.

He moved toward his SUV but her last statement nagged at him. The attackers hadn't followed her out of the building. Maybe the cops' presence scared them off, but they didn't even try to shoot at her once she entered the parking garage. Jake glanced up at Skye, who was not quite halfway to her car. The contents of Randy's accident folder rushed to the forefront of his mind.

He jogged toward her. "Skye, wait."

With a pivot, she turned. "What?"

A ball of orange exploded behind her into the night sky. Jake slammed onto the ground, the breath knocked from his lungs. He rolled onto his side and gasped for air.

Smoke drifted into the parking structure, stealing much-needed oxygen. Pebbles and concrete fragments pelted his body.

Jake army-crawled across the floor below the smoke line. Tinnitus rang in his ears, and muffled car alarms barked from the nearby street. The wind shifted, blowing clouds of soot across his path. He held his breath as bits of ash rained down and dirtied his skin. Black smoke tumbled from the blazing inferno that used to be Skye's car.

He scanned the area and spotted her body. She wasn't moving.

Sirens blared. Voices muffled together over her. Skye tried to raise her hand and remove the covering from her face, but straps restrained her arms. A hard board underneath her head intensified the ache pounding through her temples. Her entire body hurt, including pain shooting through her ribs when she inhaled.

"BP's 130/94. Pulse is 110. Respirations are stable." She didn't recognize the male voice on her left and tried to force her eyes open, but the light inside the mobile compartment intensified her headache.

"Skye, don't move. You've been hurt. You're in an ambulance, on a backboard, and the paramedics are taking us to the hospital to get checked out." Jake spoke from her right. She stretched her fingers out to him. The warmth of his hand slipped into hers.

"Romi?" she asked, her throat parched.

"I called Carli, and she's keeping her at the

ranch for the night. I'm right here with you, but we need to get you to the hospital."

She shook her head. "Home."

"You can't go home right now. Your car exploded. The doctors need to run some medical tests to make sure you don't have any internal damage."

Flashes of the explosion came back to her in waves of consciousness. She remembered heat and an intense force propelling her body across the concrete floor, then nothing until now.

The ambulance came to a stop, and her stretcher lifted and rolled. Cooler night air whisked around Skye's body, chilling her skin, despite the draped sheet covering her. More voices shouted, tossing questions at the paramedics.

"What have we got?"

"Female, twenty-seven, suffered possible internal trauma from a car explosion. Also, we need someone to take a look at Detective Reed's arm. He's got a nasty gash."

"I'm fine," Jake said. "Just take care of her."

Skye opened her eyes.

Jake walked beside her, still holding her hand, and pushing the bed toward large double doors with a bright red neon sign spelling Emergency.

She'd been here before, the night Randy had died.

Inside, nurses bustled around, sticking her

arms with needles, and placing adhesive leads on her chest.

"We're going to give you a sedative, Skye. Something to help you relax." A blonde nurse smiled at her while inserting a syringe into her IV. Monitors beeped and scents of antiseptic triggered memories from the accident. Skye let them play in her head.

Romi's favorite children's song had been playing on the radio. They sang together despite the rain pouring outside. Randy hated driving in storms and couldn't wait to get home, but he put on a smile and joined in their duet.

Bright lights, approached from the left, blinding them. Metal crunched against the driver's door, sending them into a spin. Wet dirt and debris slung around them, pitching them into a ditch on the other side of the road. Glass from Randy's window shattered, cutting his arm. He tugged on her seat belt, but the buckle stuck. He kept glancing out the driver's side window and yanking on the restraint, telling her they needed to go.

Romi screamed from the back seat, and Skye turned to comfort their daughter. The little girl didn't have a scratch on her, but she wanted out of her seat and reached toward her mother.

Skye was able to loosen her seatbelt and she saw him. A man with a skull tattoo walked toward the front of their car. Darkness shadowed his face, and bright headlights continued to glare against the rain-streaked window. She expected the man to help, to make sure they were okay, but when he stopped next to Randy, he leaned forward with his hand raised. A glint of light reflected from a knife blade, and his arm swung down with force.

Skye bolted up, gasping for breath, her eyes wide open. Monitors beeped around her, and a nurse typed information into the computer. She'd been moved from the holding area into an ER bay. The backboard and neck collar were gone, but the nightmare of Randy's death was still fresh in her mind.

Jake stepped to her side, his arm bandaged with white gauze. "You're okay. You've got a concussion, but nothing too serious. How do you feel?"

"My head hurts, but that's all. How long was I asleep?"

"For a while. The medicine knocked you out. You even slept through the CT scan. Good news—you still have a brain."

She couldn't help but smile at his weak joke. "Funny. What happened at the library?"

"Someone fastened a bomb to the undercarriage of your car. I don't even want to think what would've happened if you'd been any closer when the vehicle blew."

"Or if Romi had been with me," she said, the statement almost choking in her throat.

His gaze met hers and she let the heaviness of her words resonate between them. She needed help and couldn't do this alone, especially if she wanted to keep Romi safe.

Skye motioned for her bag, hanging on the back of the door. "There's something I need to give you."

Jake reached for her purse, then handed it to her. She pulled the children's book from the inside and gave it to him.

Jake read the cover. "I don't understand. Why are you giving me *Blue Bunny's Bonkers Birthday*?"

"I donated some books to the library after Randy died, including that one. Do you have a pocketknife?" She opened the book and lifted the appropriate flap. "Randy must've hidden this microchip some time before the accident. I didn't know about it until last week, when I finally got around to going through his home office. I found a letter in his desk telling me about the chip and to give it to Zain in the case of his death."

Jake retrieved a small knife from his pocket and slid the blade underneath the lining. "Is this why you were attacked in the library?"

"I believe so."

"Why didn't you tell me about this earlier?"

"He told me to only trust Zain with the information. Most people consider Randy's death an accident, including me, but after tonight, I'm not so sure."

The muscles in his jaw tensed with her news. "Did Randy say what was on here?"

"Nothing in the letter, but for him to hide something like this means whatever's on the chip is significant."

Jake ran a hand across the back of his neck. "Do you remember anything from the night Randy died?"

"Not much." She kept the vivid dream to herself. She had no way of knowing if the dream was real or a byproduct of the sedatives she'd been given.

He moved to the sliding glass door of her ER bay and pulled it closed. The hospital might be small but their trauma department had modern, private rooms with real walls instead of curtains dividing patient areas. He unzipped his backpack, pulled out a folder and handed it to her. "I also think this is why someone tried to kill you tonight."

She read the name printed in bold, black ink in the top left-hand corner.

Randy Anderson, deceased.

Jake sat without saying a word as Skye ran her fingers across a copied photo of Randy, attached to the inside of the file. Her chin trembled and she swiped a hand across her wet cheek before the moisture dripped on the pages.

"Where did you get this?"

"Someone left the file on my desk for review. The documents inside look like they've been copied, but when I compared it to his report in the database, the file contained extra information."

"But he's been dead for more than a year, and the crash was ruled an accident. Why would someone give this to you now?"

"Maybe because I reopened Randy's case."

Her eyes widened at his announcement. "Do you think that caused tonight's attack?"

"Could have. Randy was taken to the hospital after the accident, correct?"

"That's what I was told. I don't remember much from that night, and I didn't wake up for three days after the accident. My memories are limited."

"But do you remember what happened after the collision? Do you remember seeing anyone there?"

"Bits and pieces. A few flashes come back to me every now and then. To be honest, I try not to remember the worst night of my life."

He didn't want to cause her more pain, but if he planned to solve Randy's murder, he needed answers. The ones in the file didn't add up and prompted more questions no one at the police department had investigated.

"Look here." He pointed to the emergency department record. "They describe the edges of Randy's fatal wound as being shredded and torn."

She read the section. "One of Randy's friends told me a piece of glass embedded itself into his neck during the wreck and severed his main artery. He bled out in a few minutes. Perhaps the jagged edges from the glass created the irregularities."

Jake retrieved an image from the back of the folder. "Here's the shard of glass they found on the floor they claimed made the fatal cut. His blood is on the surface. The size of the glass is too small to have made the two-inch cut in Randy's neck. Also, the edges are smooth, sharp. If this piece of glass made the lethal cut, then the officers should've found smooth edges in the wound."

Skye closed her eyes and leaned her head back against the stretcher. Jake hadn't even considered how the images might affect her.

"Sorry. I should've warned you before whipping those out to view."

She waved a hand. "The photos actually help. The man tonight at the library had a skull tattoo inked on his arm. I remember the same tattoo from the night we wrecked which should be in my statement I gave a few days after the accident."

"What else do you remember about the man?"

She turned her gaze to his. "When I was under sedation, I dreamed the same man stabbed Randy in the neck with a knife. I figured the dream was my brain's way of coping with the trauma."

Her words confirmed Jake's theory. "I think the dream was your brain's way of uncovering the truth. And now they're coming after you."

"Who's behind this?"

He flipped to another set of documents in the file. "The last case Randy investigated involved Dante Carello. He's the kingpin of the Carello cartel and is ruthless when his business is threatened. Randy discovered his operation and called in the DEA to dismantle the network."

"The Drug Enforcement Agency was involved?"

"They sent Randy undercover to infiltrate the cartel from the inside. The information he uncovered had the power to put Dante behind bars for good."

"But why are they coming for me after all this time?"

Jake took a seat next to her and clasped his hands. "When I took this job, I had already been looking into Randy's accident. One of my goals when returning to Crystal Creek was to reopen Randy's case. His death is one of the reasons I came back. I believe Dante knows we're looking into his operation and feels threatened."

"And doing so, you put my life and Romi's at risk." Skye pulled back the covers on the bed and sat up, letting her legs dangle over the side. "I need to get out of here."

"You can't go. They haven't discharged you yet. I know this is a lot to take in, but you have to stay until the doctor clears you to leave."

Skye repositioned herself on the bed. "Romi and I have been through so much. We were starting to get our lives back to some sense of normalcy. If Dante Carello is coming after us, then I have to protect her."

"We can stop him together. Help me place him at the accident scene, and I can tie him to Randy's murder. You're the only witness we have."

"I can't help you."

"Don't you want justice for Randy?"

"Not at the expense of my daughter. And Randy wouldn't want her in harm's way, either. She's all I have left. I'll do whatever it takes to protect her, even if that means bowing out of any investigation the police have reopened."

He understood her reluctance. Skye's priority centered on Romi, but Jake wanted justice for his friend, for the man who had saved his life. He couldn't change the past, but Jake planned to hunt down Carello and make him pay for killing Randy, no matter the cost.

THREE

A wave of nausea swept through Skye at the thought of someone harming her daughter.

"You're sure Romi's safe, right?"

Jake scrolled through his phone and pulled up the previous texts he sent to Zain and Carli while she was sleeping, then showed her the screen. Skye read every one before handing the phone back to him. She didn't look convinced.

"Don't worry. Zain and Carli's property, the Moore Family Ranch, is designed to protect witnesses before trials. His security is top-notch, and Zain's offered his safe house for you and Romi to stay in when you're released from the hospital. They even said you can bring your dog."

"Sully may never leave with all that land to roam."

"You can roam with him. The relaxation may help you recover your memories from the accident." She glanced at the copied file again.

Maybe something in the pages would trigger her memory.

"Will I be able to look over these documents again?"

"Of course. I always have access to them while I'm working the case. Just let me know when you want to see them."

"Thanks. I think after a couple days at home will do me some good. Then I'd like to look over everything again."

"We can't let you go home. If Carello is coming for you, then you can guarantee he knows where you live. He's not someone you can run from, Skye. He won't stop, and he'll use whatever means necessary to get you to comply, including Romi. Zain's ranch is the safest place for both of you."

Sergeant Zain Wescott converted his family acreage into a safe haven for witnesses who agreed to testify against suspects but didn't want to enter witness protection.

"You know a lot about Dante Carello."

"Because his territory stretches into Charlotte, also. When I worked there, we raided a multitude of the gang's warehouses but were unable to stop the operation. The man wipes out entire families, women and children if anyone gets in his way."

"Does Zain think Randy's death is related to Carello?"

"He does since I reopened the case. Randy was

investigating several cases when he died, including a young woman's death Dante was tied to. Do you remember a Lorna Daly? She fell from the top of a waterfall."

"About ten years ago, right?"

"Yeah. She went hiking and apparently slipped, falling sixty feet."

"What's that have to do with Dante?"

"She was dating him at the time. The report said he had an alibi for the day she died, but I thought it was odd that Randy counted her death with the other drug-related murders he tied to Carello."

"Maybe the microchip will provide more for you to go on. I wish I could remember the man's face, but it was so dark and rainy. All I remember is the skull tattoo."

"No worries. Dr. Frye and I can work to help you remember more once you're moved to the ranch."

Skye struggled with the thought of having Jake in her life again. His presence stirred up past feelings she wasn't ready to acknowledge. Randy had been dead for a year and she loved him, but Jake still held a piece of her heart despite how he'd ended their relationship.

"I don't know about moving, Jake. Romi has already lost so much with losing her father. I don't know if she can handle losing her home, too."

His hand touched her arm and heat radiated against her skin. "These men won't stop until you're both dead. Moving to a safe location temporarily is better than losing her life forever."

He was right. Skye dismissed any reservations about her history with Jake. If staying at the ranch under lock and key kept them alive, then she'd figure out a way to handle her feelings.

"I'll need to stop by my house on the way home and pick up a few items for us."

"No problem. I'll take you once you're discharged. I promise I won't let anything happen to you or Romi."

He'd made promises before—vows to love her forever, to never leave, to give them a future—but he'd broken them all. Skye refrained from vocalizing her skepticism and forced a small smile to her face, praying he didn't let her down again. This time her daughter's life was at stake.

Isolated hallways wound through multiple areas at Crystal Creek hospital. Blank walls of cream held a few paintings from local artists, but the decor and upkeep diminished the farther one meandered from the main spaces.

Jake walked to a stairwell door, glanced over his shoulder, and entered. The door clanged behind him. He glanced up the steps, then down. No one was around.

He descended to the ground floor, walked

through another heavy metal door, and stepped outside onto a grassy bank overlooking the main four-lane road in front of the hospital. Zain leaned against the wall.

"This is your private meeting spot?" Jake asked his superior as he approached.

"Absolutely. No one's around and the traffic noise drowns out conversation. It's dark except for a few building lights. We can walk and talk around the side of the building without anyone hearing or seeing us. There's a back entrance leading to the coffee shop, which opens in ten minutes." Zain tapped his watch. "I figure at four-fifty in the morning, you could use a large cup of joe."

"I can't believe we've been here all night."

"The ER is never a quick trip."

Jake glanced around at their surroundings and inhaled the fresh, dewy air. "How did you find out about this secret entrance to the coffee shop?"

"During college I worked as a transport tech while I went to school. We learned all the ins and outs of the place and how to get to the coffee shop." He motioned around the corner to an adjoining sidewalk. "How's Skye?"

"She's sleeping and ready to go home, but I convinced her to stay. She has a mild concussion but no internal damage and a few bruised ribs from her landing. The doctor plans to discharge her after a few more hours of observation."

"Nate caught me up on the attack and explosion. Did you see anyone in the vicinity while you were talking with Skye? Any suspicious activity?"

"By the time I arrived, the bomb was already in place. Someone must have rigged her car while she was in the library. The lab is combing through the blasting caps and other debris."

"You think this is tied to Randy's death?"

Jake nodded. "The skull tattoo on Skye's attacker tonight matches the one she reported after her accident a year ago. The Carello cartel inks all their members with the same design. The attack has to be tied to Dante."

"Agreed, but Dante doesn't typically use explosives."

"So, he's changed up his MO. This is him. I'm sure of it."

"We need more evidence for a judge to give us a search warrant for Dante's estate and his warehouses. I want concrete proof so he doesn't slip through our fingers again. You need to make sure whatever the DA throws at him sticks."

"Already on it. We're having the team check all the security footage within a one-mile radius of the library, and I have tails on all of Dante's runners. Plus, we're checking in with all of our confidential informants to see if they know anything to tie him to the explosion."

"Good. Why don't you head home? I'm sure your mom will be happy to know you're not injured. The Crystal Creek gossip mill is bound to have reached her by now."

"I called and let her know I'm okay."

"How's she doing since her last spell?"

"Better. I'm glad I can be here and regulate her medications."

Jake's mother had landed in the hospital a few months ago after a diabetes scare. When Zain found her unconscious from taking too much insulin, he offered Jake the open detective position.

"I'm thankful you moved back. With your credentials and work experience, we couldn't have found a better fit," Zain said.

"Randy was the better fit."

Always had been, always would be. Randy excelled at every task put in front of him during basic law enforcement training. He was the first to be hired out of their class and moved into a detective role as soon as policy allowed. Several deputies expressed jealousy toward Randy's quick rise to the top, but not Jake. His friend worked hard and put in the time to be the best. Jake aimed to be like him.

Zain folded his arms across his chest. "Hey, no guilt allowed on my force. Okay? Randy was an amazing detective, and nothing will ever diminish his time with us, but we have to move forward. *You* have to move forward."

He wanted to believe Zain's words, but black doubt had been nagging his conscience since he'd returned to Crystal Creek. Maybe coming back to his hometown was warping his state of mind and playing too much with his emotions, but Jake renewed his resolve to honor Randy's memory and bring Dante Carello to justice.

"I'll do the best I can."

They rounded a corner, and Zain gripped a door handle, opening to a long corridor. "Your hardest task is to convince our patient to move to the ranch. Skye's a stubborn one and will want to keep Romi on familiar terrain."

"She's already argued and lost the battle. I'm taking her there after they release her."

"Really? Then you're better than I thought."

"Don't get me wrong. She wasn't happy about the idea, but the explosion helped convince her, and she remembered a bit more from the night of the accident. She said Randy was alive and trying to get her seat belt unbuckled when a man walked up to his window and stabbed him in the neck. That ties right in with the Carello drug ring."

"They must have found out he was an undercover cop and decided to silence him."

"And now they want to silence Skye, since she's the only one who can tie them to Randy's murder. If she can identify his killer's face, then we can bring down Dante for his connection to the hired gun. She's the witness who can prove Randy's death was a homicide instead of an accident."

"Honestly, I'm surprised they didn't kill them all when they had the chance. The Carellos are known for wiping out entire families."

The hallway exited into the main lobby, and the coffee bar stood to their left. The person at the front of the counter placed her order and stepped to the side. Jake smiled at the barista. "Two black coffees, please."

The young girl didn't look more than sixteen. "What do you want in them?"

"Just two black coffees."

A thin, gold hoop decorated the girl's nose, and pink hair poked out from underneath her uniform hat. "Are you sure? Because we have a variety of flavors, creamers, cinnamon, nutmeg, ginger, sprinkles, chocolate syrup, espresso shots, et cetera."

Jake stared at the board listing the options she'd spouted off in less than two seconds, like a potential auctioneer in training. "No, thanks. We keep things simple. Just two black coffees." He placed a ten-dollar bill on the counter, noting her name tag read Millie.

The woman turned to her coworker. "Anyway, like I was saying. He was hot. All muscular and tough."

Long, glittery blue nails clicked on the digital tablet in rhythm with her gum smacking. She turned back to Jake. "Speaking of hot, do you want those two coffees iced or like an inferno?"

He grabbed a couple of cardboard sleeves and placed them beside his money. "Hot."

Millie's coworker stepped up to the counter. "Did you see his tattoo?"

"Some of the best work I've seen."

Jake tried not to eavesdrop on the ladies' conversation, but their lack of discretion kept him in the loop. The vague description of their new man crush grabbed his attention.

Millie held up a shaker container. "Whipped cream or chocolate sprinkles on top?"

"Neither. Just two black coffees." He grabbed a couple of stir sticks and napkins while he waited. "I don't mean to interrupt, but this tattoo, what did it look like?"

The chatty barista glanced at his badge hanging around his neck and clammed up. "Just the usual." She punched her screen a little harder. "Tall, grande, venti or trenta?"

Jake exhaled and longed for the simple days of two choices—cream and sugar. "Tall is fine."

"Six twenty-five."

Jake slowly slid the ten-dollar bill toward her,

buying more time for the girl to share her story. "The tattoo was usual how?"

Millie shot her colleague a glance, who shrugged and returned to her mixing corner.

"He had a skull tattoo on his forearm. I thought it was cool and asked him where he got the ink done, but he didn't tell me. Finding a good artist is so hard sometimes. You know what I mean?"

Jake's body tensed with the news. "Did you see where he went?"

"Toward the emergency department."

He glanced at Zain, and they both took off running.

"Hey, what about your coffees?" Millie shouted across the lobby.

Jake didn't answer but continued through the maze of hallways toward the ER. Zain followed close on his heels. They rounded a corner. Double doors blocked the main department entrance and required an employee badge swipe to enter. Zain pressed an intercom button while Jake flashed his badge toward the camera. A loud buzz echoed in the alcove and the doors parted, allowing them entrance into the annex area. Jake dashed through the narrow opening, determined to reach Skye before the assassin did.

FOUR

Skye grew agitated while she stayed in bed, waiting. She couldn't get any sleep here not when all she wanted to do was get home to Romi and make sure her little girl was okay. Most of the night had passed with tests and blood draws to rule out any internal damage. Other than being a bit woozy, she felt fine and told the doctor. He'd promised to discharge her more than an hour ago when the CT of her head came back normal, but the process lingered.

Enough with waiting.

She removed the tape from her arm, pulled out the IV needle and added some pressure to stop the bleeding. Driving was out of the question, not only due to her concussion but because someone had turned her car into a heap of ash.

She grabbed her phone and tapped the car service app. Several vehicles popped up on her map right outside the hospital. If she took a car home, packed a bag, and headed to Carli's ranch, she could make it by the time Romi woke up. They always ate breakfast together, and she refused to let some cartel members get in the way of the tradition.

Skye swapped the flimsy hospital gown for her comfy T-shirt sullied with smoke and black ash. The scrub pants she requested bagged a bit but looked better than her torn shorts. Maybe they wouldn't miss one pair.

Someone pulled the door open, and Skye jumped. The pretty blonde nurse from before stepped into her room, holding a stack of discharge papers. "What are you doing?"

"I'm leaving."

"The doctor just finished his discharge process and if you can sign a few papers then I'll get your wheelchair to escort you to your car."

Skye took the pen and scribbled her signature on the pages presented.

"My shorts are ripped and I need to wear these pants home. I'll be happy to launder them and bring them back."

The nurse waved a hand. "We can add the charge to your bill. We have to do that often. You'd be surprised how many patients walk out with them."

"Well, they are comfy."

"Let me make one suggestion. You've got a concussion, so don't drive for at least twenty-four hours. Forty-eight, if you want to be on the safe side." She held out the papers in her hands. "These are your instructions to take home. I wanted to go over them with you but since you're in a rush, please be sure to read them thoroughly. If you start to have any of these symptoms, you need to come back to see us."

Skye took the papers. "I'm good, thanks. I don't mean to rush you, but I've got a car waiting outside."

"Let me grab a wheelchair for you. Policy states you must leave in a wheelchair. Wait right here."

More waiting.

The nurse left, and once she rounded the corner, Skye headed in the opposite direction, checking the app for the type of car scheduled to pick her up. A blue Honda Accord with a driver named Ruben popped up on the screen with his vehicle parked outside the main ER entrance.

She decided to text Jake after she was in the car. If she told him she was leaving, he'd want to escort her straight to Zain's and she really needed to make a stop by her house to pick up a few things. She was sure he would offer to pack for her, but she hated the thought of her ex-boyfriend rummaging around in her private drawers. He'd have to be satisfied to meet her at the ranch later.

Skye rounded the corner and swayed against the wall. Dizziness blurred her vision. Maybe she did need the wheelchair. A long corridor stretched out before her. She took a slow step forward and then stopped.

A large man dressed in a dark hoodie moved into the other end of the hallway. She couldn't make out his face in the shadows, but with his sleeves pushed up, the visible skull tattoo on his arm surged adrenaline through Skye.

He must've followed her from the library.

Skye turned and raced down the hall and around a corner. The blonde nurse moved toward her with the wheelchair.

"Wait. Stop. You need to…"

The woman's words faded, but Skye didn't slow down. She couldn't. Not if she wanted to escape from the man.

Heavy footsteps thumped on the tile behind her. Faster. Louder. He was getting close.

"Sir." The nurse's voice raised to a shrill level. "Stop running. Security. Someone get security."

Skye rushed into a busy work area. The young trauma doctor who had spent less than ten minutes with her straightened from behind the workstation. "Hey, you can't run through here."

His raised voice alerted two security guards nearby, but a loud crash behind her shifted their gaze. Skye glanced back. The man had run into a laundry cart, tipping it over. She kept moving toward the exit, through the narrow opening of the automatic door. With another look over her shoulder, the two guards confronted the tattooed man, stopping his pursuit.

A blue Honda parked at the curb. Skye flung open the door, slid inside and surprised the driver with her abrupt entrance.

"I'm Skye, and I need you to go."

He accelerated, the inertia pressing her back against the seat. After pulling onto the main road, he glanced in the rearview mirror. "Are you okay?"

"I'm fine. Just needed to get out of there."

"I understand. I'm not a fan of hospitals, either."

Skye looked out the back window, but the intruder never emerged. With a relieved exhale, she faced forward and let the soft jazz music playing through the car's speakers calm her nerves. The subtle scent of pine air freshener filled the interior of the Honda, and she took one of the peppermints in a small tray beside her. The wrapper crinkled as she opened the candy and popped the piece into her mouth.

"The address you entered into the app is 1071 Walnut Drive? Is that correct?"

"Yeah, and if we hurry, there's an extra twenty in it for you."

She pulled the bill from her bag and flashed it in the mirror. He smiled.

"You realize that's a convenient store, right?"

With the threat of danger lurking around every

corner, she planned to stop at the store and sur-
veil her nearby house for a few minutes instead
of having the car drop her at the front stoop.
"Sure do."

"Okay, as long as you know where you're
going. Buckle up and I'll do the best I can to get
you there quickly."

Skye snapped her seat belt, relaxed, and closed
her eyes. The last ten hours blurred with the
adrenaline crash from the day, and the familiar
burn of tears stung the corners of her eyes.

Jake was right. Someone had murdered Randy.
For a year, she'd believed his death was an accident, a random occurrence of bad timing and
poor judgment on their part. But there was no
denying facts anymore, particularly after the attacks on her life tonight.

Randy had uncovered a dangerous operation,
run by Dante Carello. The gang had killed her
husband, and if she didn't trust God to protect
her, she and Romi might be their next victims.

All the precinct detectives—some of whom
were Randy's best friends—believed the offi-
cial record of events and even had convinced her
there was no evidence of foul play. They never
once had questioned Randy's death as anything
other than an unfortunate collision. The officer at the scene, Clayton Bean, one of Randy's
teammates, had arrived first and recorded all the
information. When he'd visited her after she re-

turned home, he never mentioned a connection to the Carellos.

Skye opened her eyes and leaned forward. "Can I ask you something?"

The driver glanced at her. "Sure."

"If you had a chance to provide justice for a friend, but by doing so, it might put your family at risk, would you cooperate?"

"I don't know. Depends on how close I was to the friend who needed justice."

"Actually, he wasn't just any friend. He was my best friend—and husband. He died in an accident."

The man eyed her for a moment then looked back to the road. "Then yes. If anyone harmed my wife, I'd do everything to bring the person who hurt her to justice."

"Would you work with an ex to accomplish the task?"

He hit the blinker light to take her exit off the interstate. "Well, that makes the situation much more interesting. But yeah, even if I had to work with an ex-girlfriend, as long as she was the nice one, I'd do it."

"You broke things off with a nice lady?"

"After much groveling, she took me back and we've been married for thirty years. What about you? Is your ex nice?"

A short laugh escaped her lips. "I'm not sure the word *nice* describes him. He's different, can be kind when he wants to be and is well-known for his thorough investigative skills."

"Do you trust him?"

His question permeated to her soul. "With my life."

"Then there's your answer. Sounds like he wants to do what's right."

Jake always did what was right—except when the choices came to their relationship. But with Randy's case, he was the only detective to uncover new information others missed because they accepted the obvious. Randy often had spoken of Jake's tenacity when working an investigation. Her husband would get stuck on a case and call his buddy for advice. Jake always had a way to get the information Randy needed. Now, the time had come for her to work with him to find Randy's killer.

Jake had pointed out the glaring discrepancies in the medical and police reports. Had the officers missed the clear markers of her husband's death? Or worse, had one of Randy's teammates covered up the evidence?

She pulled out her phone and scrolled to Jake's number. Her finger hovered over the screen, reluctant to receive a scolding for leaving the hospital without him.

"Are you going to call him?" the driver asked.

"I don't know."

If Skye wanted to uncover the truth of Randy's

death, then she had to partner with Jake. He was the only one she trusted enough to lead the investigation. But he was also the one man who'd broken her heart.

Jake reached Skye's room first and rushed inside. Scents of bleach and antiseptic hit him like a wall, and crisp, unwrinkled white sheets dressed the stretcher, ready for a new patient. Used bags of fluid and tubing filled a red container marked with a biohazard sign. A member of the housekeeping staff wiped the counters and cleaned the chairs while the nurse stood in the corner, entering data into the electronic medical record.

"Where did the female patient assigned to this room go?"

The nurse shot him a quick glance but kept working. "I can't discuss any patient information with you."

Jake took out his badge. "How about now?"

"Sorry. HIPAA."

"I understand about not wanting to violate privacy laws, but this lady's in danger. Can you at least tell me if she left by herself?"

The nurse straightened and looked at his badge again. "She did leave by herself."

"Did you see another man, about six feet, 250 pounds, with a skull tattoo on his arm, come into the room?"

"He didn't come into the room, but he rushed past me in the hallway. He almost knocked me right into the wheelchair I brought for her, but a couple of officers stopped him at the door. As for the woman, she left via a car service."

Jake glanced at his phone. A call from Skye registered in his log, but she'd left no message. He moved into the corridor and pressed her number, but her voice mail picked up. "Skye, call me when you get this." He turned toward Zain. "At least the attacker missed her, too."

"I'll have Nate pull the security footage and talk to the guards. If they let the guy go, then we can at least get a sketch of his face. Any idea where Skye went?"

"Home to pack and then to your ranch. She'll go to Romi."

Jake's phone rang with Skye's name displayed on the screen. He tapped Accept. "Where are you?"

"I'm headed back to the house to pack a bag for me and Romi, then on to the ranch."

Jake waved a hand at Zain and headed for the door. "I'll meet you at your house. Don't leave until I get there. Our suspect followed you to the hospital, and you're in danger."

"I know. I saw him."

Jake hit the key fob to his SUV and slid into the driver's seat. "Did you get a look at him?"

"Not really. He chased me out. Thankfully, I

left when I did, or the outcome would've been different. He followed me down the hallway, but I lost him after that."

"Good. I'll be at your house in about fifteen minutes. Stay put until I get there. Lock the doors. Don't turn on a bunch of lights. If he drives by, he needs to think no one's home."

"Got it."

"Skye…be careful. He's dangerous. I'll text you when I get there."

Jake understood Skye's need to shield her daughter from any harm. Many times, his mother had tried to protect him from his father or hide him in a safe spot. His secret place was a tree house Randy's dad built in between their two properties. Sometimes his mother brought sleeping bags for the night or a few graham crackers, marshmallows, and chocolate bars if she had them. She'd done her best to protect him when he was little, but she was no match for his father. At least the man had given Jake one skill he found useful—the ability to fight against giants much larger than himself.

FIVE

The small convenience store near Skye's house opened at six in the morning, according to the yellow sign. She'd been in the building a few times when she ran out of milk or Romi wanted a Popsicle on a hot summer day. Her home wasn't far from the place, but she didn't want the driver to know her exact location.

The man rolled down his window when she stepped from the car and into the parking lot. "Are you sure this is where you want me to leave you?"

"Yeah. I'll be fine."

"This isn't the safest part of town for a woman to be alone."

"Thanks for the concern, but I'm fine. I might even grab a few things from inside." She motioned toward the entrance of the small store.

"But the place isn't open yet. I don't want to leave you alone with no one around."

"I don't live far from here." She glanced at her

watch. "Looks like they open in a little while and I know the owner, so I'm good."

"If you insist." The driver waved goodbye, rolled up his window, and pulled back onto the main road. Once he was out of sight, Skye jogged across the street and hiked a mile up her gravel driveway. Her white farmhouse came into view when she rounded the curve.

She stepped into the tree line at the edge of her property and examined the entrances. Each door remained closed. Shadows danced against the exterior walls, but no unfamiliar cars were parked in her driveway. She sprinted to the back door. A loud bark from inside echoed when she inserted the key and pushed the door open.

"Shh...boy." Her golden retriever, Sully, danced around her legs at her arrival. "Did you think I forgot about you?"

Sully had a fenced-in backyard with a large doggie door for his convenience, but he never liked being alone for too long. She poured a scoop of food into his bowl, which he gobbled up way to fast.

Randy used to take care of him, feeding him every day, but with her husband gone, the dog followed her everywhere. His presence provided her with a sense of nostalgia, comfort, and extra security. He was her pillow when her loneliness became unbearable at night or gave her kisses when all she wanted to do was cry. For a retired drug dog who had completed 372 drug busts during his tenure with the police department, Sully was the best friend a girl could have.

"We've got to pack, ole boy. Carli said you could come to the ranch, too. There's a big pasture where you can run around and chase all kinds of wild critters. Would you like that?"

The dog whined and rubbed against her for more scratches.

Skye stood and reached for the light switch but stopped. Jake had told her to keep the lights off and make the house look like no one was home. The faint daylight emerging from behind the hills wasn't enough to illuminate the rooms. Instead, she pulled a flashlight from the side table drawer and headed upstairs to her bedroom, with Sully tagging along right behind her.

The large walk-in closet held more boots than clothes. A lady could never have too many boots. She shoved her winter clothes to one side, pulled out Romi's princess suitcase and her larger rolling bag, then tossed them on her king-size bed, filling them to the brim with enough clothes to last them for months, even sweaters for when the seasons grew cooler.

Skye reached for her purse and pulled out the children's book from the library. Romi deserved to snuggle in her own bed at night and read her book or play on her tire swing instead of running for her life.

At least they'd be together, unlike Skye and her mother. Jamie Anderson had abandoned Skye when she was twelve. She still struggled with her mother's absence and didn't understand how a woman could ditch her own flesh and blood or why God allowed such heartache in the first place.

The thought pressed her to her knees, and she burst into painful sobs.

"Please keep us safe, God. I can't lose my daughter, too. I'll never survive."

A bright light flooded her bedroom through the backyard window. Sully trotted over and barked. She pulled her phone from her pocket, opened her security camera app and zoomed in on the image. Something had tripped the motion sensors. *Please be the neighbor's cat.*

A shadowed figure moved across her yard, toward the back porch. Hot rage filled her. How dare he come for her again at her home? Skye crossed the room, retrieved her Glock from the lockbox in the closet and stood to the side of the window. She disengaged the safety and racked the slide, trying to get a better view of the man skulking around her yard.

Sully perched right by her feet, waiting for her signal. The old dog remembered his training, and Skye practiced often with him. He'd attack anyone with one specific motion of her hand.

The kitchen doorknob rattled. Skye eased down the steps and gestured for Sully to move next to the front door while she covered the back. If the intruder entered through either door, she or Sully would put him down.

The outside light snapped off.

Darkened shadows provided cover as she peeked out for a better view. Light footsteps stepped across the porch, and the shadowed man looked through the window. Skye flattened against the wall and slipped her finger over the trigger, keeping both hands on the grip. Two raps knocked on the sliding door.

She didn't move.

Her phone vibrated with a message.

I'm outside.

Jake.

Adrenaline released the tension holding her muscles captive. She stepped from her hiding place and unlocked the door. "You scared me to death. I thought you said you were going to text when you first got here."

"I did." Jake locked the door behind him and petted Sully between the ears.

She held up her phone. "I only got one message, just now."

Jake tapped his screen. "Looks like the first

one failed to go through. Sorry. I must've been in a dead zone."

"There's several of those out here in the boon-docks." She waved a hand toward the stairs. "I'm almost done with the packing, and then I'll be ready to go."

Jake followed her to the second level and into her bedroom. Skye closed Romi's suitcase and filled hers with more shorts, T-shirts, and flip-flops. She moved into the bathroom to get their toothbrushes, calling back over her shoulder, "I'll need something to drive to work."

He followed her to the bathroom door. "Work's not an option right now."

Her post office job paid her bills and kept a roof over their heads. She pushed past him back to her bed. "I have to work, Jake. I can't pay my mortgage if I don't. This is Romi's home, too, and I won't let some crazed killer steal the one thing Randy left his daughter."

"They've been following you. They know your routine and won't think twice about showing up at the post office in an effort to silence you."

"What are they going to silence? I don't re-member who killed my husband. The only thing I've given you is an arm with a skull tattoo on the man who stabbed him. There are millions of men with skull tattoos. It's not really the prover-bial nail in the coffin to put a drug dealer away for life."

"I think you know more than you remember. If you hadn't seen the killer's face, then he wouldn't be targeting you."

She straightened and faced him, his body inches from hers. The light scent of his spiced cologne returned her to summer days they'd spent together while dating. "What if I didn't see his face?"

"Then we go with the sketch from the guards, the make and model of the truck. Anything to connect the assassin to the scene."

"I'm not sure I want to remember. After the crash, grief consumed me. Zain and Carli helped with Romi, took care of Sully, and nurtured my broken soul. People from church kept my refrigerator filled with food—not that I was hungry. Pounds dropped from my body. Mom always said grief—although an unhealthy option—was the best diet. Had it not been for my friends and my faith in God, I'm not sure I would be here today."

He brushed her cheek with the backs of his fingers, gentle against her skin. "You're stronger than you think, Skye. You can do this."

A rush of heat coursed through her, vanquishing any reluctance to feel his touch. Every motion slowed as if nothing else around them existed. The increased pulse of her heart took her breath and removed any inhibitions or wisdom learned from her past. His gaze fell to her lips, and he leaned toward her. She wanted to give in to him, to feel the desire of his embrace, but vast memories of his absences returned and squelched the moment.

Skye pressed a hand against his chest and pushed him back. "Don't."

He stepped away and moved toward the door. "I'm sorry. I shouldn't have."

She didn't want things to be awkward between them, but her heart couldn't take any more pain. "We had our chance, Jake. When you left for Charlotte, you made it clear you weren't marriage material. I'm guessing your mind hasn't changed."

He placed his hand on the doorknob, his voice clear. "No."

Skye slumped onto the edge of the bed, picking up one of her shirts that needed folding. "Then while we work on Randy's case, let's keep our time together professional. Romi's my life. She means everything to me, and I won't allow anyone to hurt her."

A tense movement spread through his jaw, and his blue eyes flashed. "Understood. I'll be downstairs."

Without another word, he left the room. The familiar sting of abandonment burned the corners of her eyes. Better a little pain now than more later. She never wanted to return to the depression she'd endured after he departed, that had left her in pieces.

Loneliness squatted in the corners of her heart, like an old friend comfortable being the center of attention. She'd grown used to the solitude, but God's strength never left her. Even after Randy's death, a steady, overwhelming peace carried her through the darkest days of her life. Energy didn't come from her own efforts. God battled her weakness and His power would keep her from fading when Romi needed her most.

Jake descended the stairs, shoved through the back screen door onto the porch and drank in the brisk morning air. Hues of orange and pink streaked the early sky with the rise of the sun, and the slam of the screen door dispersed a flock of house wrens from the porch rafters. Another day, another mistake.

He knew better than to try to kiss Skye. His impulsive decisions broke every rule he'd established to keep from crossing a professional line. Something about seeing her again and spending time together threw off his better judgment.

There was no way Jake could ever live up to Randy's example. Even in death, the entire town loved his best friend, but Jake had always been damaged goods. He wasn't husband or father material, a fact his dad had always pointed out.

He had given her up. Not only for his career,

but for Randy. His best friend had loved her, too. He never said the words, but Jake knew.

Randy and his family had taken Jake under their wings, had given him a place to live while his mom got the help she needed. They'd saved his life and his family.

He'd already stepped into Randy's job at the sheriff's office and trying to kiss his widow crossed a line. The sooner he took down Dante, the sooner he could head back to Charlotte and leave his past behind.

Jake grabbed his phone and dialed Nate's number. "Do we have the report about the explosive device found at the library?"

"The lab doesn't open until eight, and they need more time than one day to test all the debris we found at the crime scene. With all the fragments from Skye's car and the rubble from the parking garage, the report could take weeks, maybe months if other cases are in front of ours."

Jake paced to the edge of the porch and scanned the perimeter of the trees, replaying the explosion in his mind. "I know. I wish things moved faster in this town."

"A nice thought, Detective Big City, but probably ain't gonna happen anytime soon."

"What about the security footage from the library and the hospital? I remember a van parked across the street in a gravel lot. I didn't think much about it then, but now—"

"You think the vehicle belonged to our suspects?"

Jake pinched the bridge of his nose, commanding his brain to think. "They'd have a good vantage point from there and be well within range to detonate the pipe bomb when Skye got near her car. If we could match it to a vehicle at the hospital and grab a plate, we might be able to bring one of them in on charges."

"I'll pull all the security footage from the cameras in and around the library from earlier in the day and go through the hospital parking footage also. Maybe we'll get a match."

"Make sure to go back several hours before the explosion. They had to plant the explosive on her car before going inside. We need a face on camera."

"Don't worry. We'll get them."

"Yeah. Sooner rather than later, I hope."

The sound of Nate tapping laptop keys filtered through the phone. "How's Skye?"

"She's as good as can be expected."

The typing noise stopped. "I'm sure this can't be easy for either one of you with your history."

"Yeah. She mentioned our breakup a few minutes ago. She still has some hard feelings."

"Well, you did leave her for your job."

He shuffled his foot across a board. "You and I both know the real reason I left. Randy loved her, and I owed him my life. She wanted more than I could give."

"And now?"

Jake turned and faced the house, leaning against the railing. "We both know I'm not the family-man type."

"People change. Maybe you should give the idea some consideration. So what if your father was cruel? That doesn't mean you will be."

Jake wasn't so sure. Too many times rage ran through him toward the criminals who beat their wives and children. He longed to give them a taste of their own medicine, seek revenge in his own way. The desire for violence ran strong through his DNA.

"After all we've seen, how do you stay so optimistic, Nate? We break up abusive situations weekly. Every time I walk into one of those homes and see the bruises on the victims, my past rushes back. I don't want to bring leftover baggage into an already-made family. Skye and Romi deserve so much more than what I have to give, but the one way I can help them is to solve this case."

"I'll tell ya what I'll do. I'll call my friend Joyce down in the lab. She owes me a favor. Let me see if I can get your explosives report moved up a few."

"Thanks, man. I appreciate it. Call ya later."

Jake ended the call as the screen door squeaked

open, and Skye emerged, pulling two suitcases behind her, followed by Sully. The dog wasn't letting her out of his sight.

"Okay, I think that's everything," she said.

Jake lifted the bags and placed them in his SUV while Skye put Sully in the back, then climbed into the passenger seat. "Nice vehicle. Is it yours?"

"The department's, but it's assigned to me while I'm here."

"While you're here? Are you thinking of leaving again?"

Jake turned on the radio, hoping the constant noise might keep more questions at bay. "Not any time soon. Mom needs me right now."

They rode in silence until they hit the main road. Skye pressed a couple of the buttons on the console, checking out the features of his ride. "I've been meaning to ask you about the remodel of your home. How's the progress going?"

"Slow, but I think the improvements will make life easier for her, plus I've added extra security with interior and exterior cameras around the property. I can keep an eye on her when I'm at work. If she falls, the camera sends an alarm to my phone."

"So Big Brother really is watching. Does she not mind being on camera all the time?"

"She's good with the changes. Sometimes she even waves at me or tells me something over the camera. Ever since her diabetes worsened, she's been a fall risk. When she lived alone, her medicine got out of sync. I make sure she takes the right dosage every day. Hopefully we won't have any more incidents."

Jake slowed the car and turned into a wide driveway. Black metal gates opened, welcoming them onto the Moore Family Ranch. Two men with weapons at their sides stood sentry at the gatehouse and waved them through.

He drove past the main house and two barns, then pulled up next to a guest home on the other side of a small cave entrance. Crystal Creek ran at the back of the property. "Home sweet home— for the foreseeable future, anyway."

"I'm so thankful to Zain and Carli for letting us stay here. Wasn't this his grandmother's home?"

Jake climbed from the vehicle and joined her. They peered up at the two-story white clapboard house. "I believe so. She used to make the best cookies for us when we came over to swim."

"I remember those. Oatmeal raisin. Zain brought me a huge batch after my mom split and then for every birthday after until I turned eighteen."

Skye's dysfunctional family history had bonded them together in their early teens. She used to talk about missing her mom, and he'd discussed his feelings about his father. He wasn't sure which was worse—to feel unwanted by the person who gave you life or to be beaten by the man who was supposed to protect his family.

They moved to the back of the SUV, and Jake opened the hatch. "Remember when she packed Zain a big box and we hiked up to Crystal Creek falls to go swimming in the lower lagoon?"

"I loved hiking up there—until Lorna Daly slipped and fell from the top. The park rangers closed the entrance after her death."

"Until a few years ago. They reopened the space and erected signs everywhere, plus put up a chain-link fence bordering the trail. Of course, kids still climb over it."

"I haven't been up there in years," she said, her gaze wistful.

Jake set the suitcases on the gravel drive and looked at her. "Since the night we ended our relationship."

"Don't you mean the night *you* ended our relationship." Her emphasis struck a nerve.

"Fair enough."

The front door of the safe house suctioned open, interrupting the awkward moment. Romi walked onto the porch with Carli behind her. Sully bounded from the vehicle and ran circles around Romi, licking her cheek. Their family was back together.

"Mommy." The little girl wore her pajamas

and lifted her arms, a ragged blue blanket capturing the early-morning breeze.

Jake watched Skye sweep her daughter into her arms and smother her in kisses. High-pitched giggles echoed across the yard.

"She didn't sleep very well last night and woke up around five o'clock this morning with a bad dream. She's still quite tired," Carlie said.

"That makes two of us." Skye gave her daughter another hug, rubbing her back with her fingers, then set her back onto the porch, keeping her close to her side.

Jake's mother used to do the same to him. So many times, she'd tried to give him the love he craved from his father. Picnics down by the creek or pushes on the tire swing provided a few good memories. She took him on nature walks after dinner, and if they timed their return correctly, his father was already passed out, in an unwakeable stupor. Those nights they were safe.

Jake closed the SUV's rear hatch, carried the two suitcases into the home and placed them in the foyer. He scanned the small space. An open living and kitchen area greeted guests with an overstuffed couch and a couple of armchairs. Stairs ascended in front of him to a landing with bedrooms off each side. Ivory candles filled the white brick fireplace on the wall to his right, and an enclosed sunroom located at the rear of the kitchen provided an area for the guards to stay. His rotation was tonight.

Candyce Frye, Crystal Creek's town physician, emerged from the hallway, wiping her hands on a paper towel. Skye entered and stood beside him, stopping midstride at the woman's presence. Her smile faded.

"Dr. Frye? What are you doing here?"

"Jake asked me to talk to you, see if we could schedule some time together."

Skye's posture stiffened next to his and she rested a hand on Romi's head. "I need to get settled in first, and I planned to spend the day with my daughter. This really isn't a good time."

"No worries." Candyce slipped a business card from her purse, shot Jake a look, then handed her contact information to Skye. "Call me once you're comfortable and I can swing back by."

Jake opened the door for her. "Thanks for coming on short notice."

"Anytime." Candyce exited the home, and Skye turned to Carli. "Can you take Romi and get her some juice in the kitchen? I need a moment with Jake."

When her daughter was out of earshot, Skye leveled a sharp gaze on him. "What were you thinking? I never gave you permission to talk to Candyce without my approval."

"I need you to remember more details. You hold the pieces to finding this guy. I can't arrest him for Randy's murder without you. If we fail and this guy gets away, you and Romi will never be safe."

Skye opened the front door. "Well, I'm not going to remember anything more today, and the truth is, I'm exhausted. I'm going to take Romi upstairs for a nap and then maybe I'll be able to function—or, better yet, remember something new."

"Don't be mad. I want what's best for you and your daughter."

Her demeanor softened. "I know. I'm just tired. That's all."

"We both are. I'll head home for a bit to check on my mom, eat and grab some shut eye. I'll be back for the night rotation."

Her eyebrows arched with his announcement. "You're staying here? Tonight?"

"Not in the safe house, but on the enclosed back sunroom. Another officer will be stationed out front during the day. We can't take any chances with your safety."

"Because of Dante Carello?"

He didn't want to scare her, but she needed to understand the gravity of the situation.

"They'll stop at nothing to silence you. Guards will be with you at all times, even if Romi wants to play outside. When you're in the house, they'll be stationed at the doors and provide a perimeter check around the home every thirty minutes. If you decide to go anywhere, they must go with you. Do you understand?"

Her eyes widened, and she gave a quick nod. The parameters might seem a bit extreme to her, but Jake had witnessed Dante's murderous tendencies. He wasn't taking any chances with Skye or Romi's safety.

SIX

Jake opened the door to the mudroom of his home. Scents of coffee, bacon and scrambled eggs greeted him when he stepped inside the kitchen along with the sizzle of meat frying in a pan. He peeked around the corner. "Got enough for me?"

His mother turned and gave him a kiss on the cheek. "Of course I do. I figured you would be hungry after the night you had. I appreciate the text, by the way. Did you see my response?"

She always amused him when tackling new technology. "I did."

"I'm getting better, don't you think?"

"You're a natural, Mom."

She smiled and turned back to the stove. "How's Skye doing?"

"Well, she's got a gash on her head and a concussion from the explosion, but she's safe for the moment. She's being guarded at the ranch."

"At least they have a little space to roam outdoors."

"I'm not sure the great outdoors will satisfy Skye. She wants nothing more than to be in her own home with her daughter, but at least she's cooperating for now."

"And how are you? It can't be easy working so close to the love of your life." His mother placed several slices of bacon beside a heap of scrambled eggs and handed him the plate. She'd always had a way of bringing up difficult topics as a side dish.

"Skye isn't the love of my life."

"Don't lie to me, boy. A mother knows when her son loves someone."

"Doesn't matter. Our relationship ended a long time ago."

"A lot of awful things ended a long time ago, but your feelings for Skye aren't among them." She placed a hand over his heart. "Don't let your father's sins ruin the good God has for you."

Jake crunched a piece of bacon. He believed in God, but the God he knew seemed to dole out more punishment than good.

His mom refilled his coffee cup. "You know, you're not him. Not even close. And you deserve to find joy and love, too."

"I love you, Mom. Thanks."

"I love you, too." She leaned forward and kissed his head. "I just want what's best for you.

I'm not getting any younger, you know, and I want to make sure you're not alone when I go live with Jesus."

"You don't need to worry about me. I'll be fine." Jake downed the last of his coffee. "I'm going to grab some sleep before heading back to the ranch for guard duty tonight, but I'll make sure to fill your pill box before I leave."

"And I'll be praying, and the Lord will be working."

He wasn't sure about the latter part of her statement. God had always seemed to be working against Jake his entire life, but out of respect for his mother, he kissed her cheek and headed upstairs for a morning nap without any disagreement.

Rain streaked down large windows in the safe house's main living area and bounced off the concrete sidewalk leading to the driveway. A haze covered the fields of the Moore Family Ranch, which were empty of any livestock after the first clash of thunder rumbled.

Skye plopped into an overstuffed armchair while she waited for her daughter to wake up from her late-afternoon nap turning into an evening slumber. She might have to rouse her from dozing in a few minutes so the little girl would sleep tonight, especially after the morning nap they'd also taken. Romi hadn't slept this much since she was two.

These were the moments she missed Randy the most. Quiet evening times they used to share snuggling in bed or laughing at each other's jokes. Sometimes he even played music, took her in his arms and swayed to the rhythm. He'd spin her around, tell her how beautiful she was and dance until they broke into giggles over his two left feet. She hadn't danced since his death.

Skye lifted her hot tea and took a sip, then refocused on her notepad. The list of memories took up a few lines. She'd hoped to remember more from the night of the accident, since the weather conditions had been similar to the current storm pummeling the roof.

She closed her eyes. Glares from oncoming headlights had blinded Randy in the darkness, but he kept driving, eager to get home after Romi's horse-riding lessons. They sang to the radio and tried to keep their daughter from focusing on the scary storm outside. The rest of the night became one big blur.

God, help me remember.

A knock rapped on the door, returning her to the present moment, and she bolted upright.

"Ms. Anderson?" The officer peeked his head around the door. "Dr. Candyce Frye is here to see you."

The pint-size woman dressed in designer clothes

and heels shook the rain from her coat. "It's a monsoon out there."

"Forgive me, but did we have something scheduled?" Skye asked.

"No, and I should've called first, but driving in six o'clock traffic is a bear, and with this torrential downpour I doubt you could've heard me anyway." Candyce smiled at the guard as he stepped back to his post and closed the door, leaving the two women alone.

"Please have a seat." Skye motioned toward the couch.

"Thanks. It is a mess out there."

"Would you like a hot cup of tea?"

"That would be lovely. Where's Romi?"

Skye lifted her own empty mug, headed into the small open kitchen, and poured them both a fresh cup. "She's taking another nap. Poor little thing was tuckered out and if I don't get her up soon, she won't sleep tonight."

"You both have been through so much lately. That's why I decided to drop by."

Skye moved back into the sitting area and handed the tea to her guest.

"Thank you." Candance wrapped her manicured fingers around the base. "I know this isn't easy, but I can help. Together we can get the information Jake needs and return you and Romi back to your home sooner rather than later. Isn't that what you want?"

Skye did want to be home again, in her own space with her daughter. Maybe Candyce could help. If talking with this woman reinstated normalcy in her life and work, then what harm could come from trying? After all, she had asked God to help her remember.

"Fine. But if I say the word, we end the session."

"Deal."

Candyce took a sip from her mug, then motioned for Skye to follow her onto the enclosed sunporch and offered her a comfortable, cushioned patio chair. "I thought the sound of rain on the tin roof out here might help return you to the night inside your car."

"You're right. It sounds the same. Except there was children's music playing on the stereo."

"What was the name of the song?" Candyce retrieved her phone and tapped an app.

"A song about Zacchaeus."

"Is this it?" She hit Play.

"Close enough."

"Great. Now, close your eyes and walk me through all the details, even the small ones."

Skye did as she instructed. "Randy drove down a dark stretch of two-lane road, leading to the back side of our home."

"Why didn't he take the interstate? Why did he take that road home?"

"There were several wrecks on I-26 and it was a parking lot."

Skye shifted her body toward the right. She'd been looking out the passenger window. "Randy hated driving on rainy nights. The glare of on-coming cars hurt his eyes. Mine, too. The thunder and lightning popping around us scared Romi, so we turned on her children's music CD and sang along. I remember looking out at the tall grass in the fields, lining the road and waving in the storm."

Skye stood, moved to the window, and breathed deeply to quiet her heart as the memories rushed into her mind.

"The headlights came from the left."

"Do you see the truck?"

"Only the bright lights. By the time I turned, metal crunched and sent us spinning. The force pinned me against the door, and then we slammed into something. Maybe a bank or even a tree. I hit my head on the window with the impact. The airbag hit me with a strong force and pressed against me. I tried to look at Randy to make sure he was okay. My vision blurred, making two of every object. Romi screamed in the back seat, much louder than the children's song still playing on the stereo. I tried to turn to her and make sure she was okay, but the locked seat belt kept me fastened into position."

"Did Randy say anything?"

"He wanted us to get out of the car and kept pulling on my seat belt. I tried to tell him we needed to stay until the cops came, but I struggled to get the right words out. Probably from my head injury."

"Could you see over the airbag?"

"I pushed the bag down, and bright headlights glared through the darkness highlighting the rain pelting off the hood. A large, shadowed figure, ripped with muscles, walked toward Randy's side of the car. At first I thought he was coming to help, but then a beam of light reflected off his blade."

"What did Randy do?"

"He kept tugging on the buckle and insisted we had to get out of here, but the belt didn't give. He continued glancing at the man stalking toward us. The guy wore a hoodie with its sleeves pushed up. The glare hid his facial features, but I could see the skull tattoo on his forearm."

"What else?"

"That's when I faded. My eyes were so heavy, and my head ached. I closed my eyes, but Randy yelled at me to stay awake. I looked again, I saw the man's arm lift and then the knife blade sank into Randy's neck. I wanted to scream and help Randy, but my body wouldn't move or respond. The next thing I remember is waking up in the hospital."

A streak of lightning stretched across the night

sky as Candyce joined her at the window. "Go back to when you looked out over the airbag, over the rain pelting off the hood. Were you able to see anything identifying the truck parked in front of you?"

Skye closed her eyes again. "There was a parking sticker in the window on the passenger side."

"Do you recognize the design?"

"A horse jumping over poles."

"Only one local place breeds and trains competition horses to jump over poles," a male voice said behind them.

Skye turned, not having realized Jake had entered during her discussion with Candyce. He leaned against the door frame and kept his gaze on her.

"Where?" she asked.

"The Cavanaugh Equestrian Center."

"Bryn Cavanaugh's business? I grew up with her, and she's one of the kindest women I know. Their business and event center is known worldwide for their competitions and racehorses. Plus, they loved Randy. Why would they be associated with the man who killed him?"

"I didn't say it was Bryn, but it could have been one of the hundreds of employees who work for them. We need to find out if she runs background checks on her staff before they're hired and have her provide a list so we can cross-reference their vehicles to the truck."

"Sounds like my work tonight is done." Candyce lifted her purse and held out a business card to Skye.

"You gave me one already."

The woman smiled. "Sorry. Professional habit. We can meet again in a few days. Give me a call with your schedule."

"Thanks."

The porch door swung closed, and jitters radiated through Skye. She glanced at Jake, who was still leaning against the interior door frame. They were alone again—and the last time they'd been alone, he'd tried to kiss her.

With a small smile, he moved to the couch, fluffed the pillow, and kept his distance.

She wasn't ready to tackle whatever was stirring between them. "I guess we need to go see Bryn tomorrow and tell her about your theory."

"We will, but there's something else I want to try."

"What?"

"Were you able to make out the man's face from the hospital?"

Skye didn't want to disappoint him, but the man had worn a hoodie that shadowed his face. "I don't think I saw enough. The pain meds blurred my vision. When I saw the tattoo on his arm, I ran out. What about the guards? Didn't they stop him?"

"They tried, but he escaped. They didn't get

a good look at his face, either." He stretched his long legs across the length of the couch. "No worries. Maybe if we go back to the accident site, some of your memories will return."

Skye often took the long way around instead of driving down the two-lane road where Randy had died. The deserted area gave her the creeps. "Isn't being out in the open dangerous?"

"I'll go with you. Nothing to fear."

Except the fear of spending too much time alone with Jake. She trusted him to protect her physically, but every moment with him tore at her heart.

SEVEN

Hundreds of competitors were preparing for the jumping competition at the Cavanaugh Equestrian Center. Young men and women wore navy blue riding coats, khaki pants, and leather boots while walking their horses to and from the ring. Wealthy sponsors and trainers filled every nook, hoping to find their next champion. Jake stood beside Skye, who held Romi's hand and smiled when her daughter pointed her finger at every "pony" passing by.

He kept his eyes open for Bryn Cavanaugh. The sticker on the window of the truck Skye had seen led back to her family's facility and Jake hoped the woman might be able to offer some clarity regarding the man trying to kill Skye.

"There she is." Skye pointed past the main entrance to the other side of the event center. Bryn wore a dark suit and waved when she saw them.

"Let's go see if she knows a man with a skull tattoo."

They wound their way across the floor and Jake shook the woman's hand in greeting, then followed her upstairs to an office overlooking the arena below. Large one-way windows framed the entire riding event space and provided a great spectator view.

Bryn paced across the room toward a small cabinet area. "Can I offer you something to drink? Water, soda, tea?"

"None for me." Jake sat down in a chair at a small conference table.

"Skye?"

"I wouldn't mind having a bottled water for Romi." She steered her daughter to a nearby play area with toys.

The woman opened a small refrigerator and passed one to her friend. "Your daughter's getting so big. I really need to bring Oscar over for a playdate."

"We'd love that." Skye poured the water into a sippy cup and handed it to her daughter. "It's been too long since we've gotten together."

"I agree, but you've had so much going on. Walter told me about your attack and the explosion. I'm glad you're okay."

Jake pulled out a security photo he'd retrieved from the hospital monitors and slid the enlarged image across to Bryn. "That's one of the reasons we are here. Have you ever seen this man?"

Bryn studied the picture for a moment and

then passed it back. "I don't think so. It's hard to see his face with the hoodie on, but nothing else about him looks familiar."

He handed her another photo of the equestrian center sticker Skye had described from her memory. "What about this?"

"Sure. We give parking stickers to all our employees and annual pass holders for security purposes. Looks like that one is at least a couple of years old. We change the design a little bit every year to help the security team identify disgruntled former employees looking to return with nefarious purposes in mind."

Jake tapped the photo of the man. "Do you think he could be one of your former employees?"

Bryn studied the image again. "Maybe. We hire hundreds of people, especially during competition season, and many of them are temporaries. We also hire college-age students in the summer who leave when they head back to school. He doesn't look like one of our full-time staff, though. Do you have a better angle to see his face?"

"I wish I did. Do you keep a record of all your employees' names?"

"We enter everyone into a database. I can have my assistant print a list for you if you want."

"That would be helpful. Are there any features on the sticker to differentiate between a pass holder and an employee?"

Bryn took the photo again, opened a magnifier on her phone and studied the image. "Looks like this was one of our employees. See the number at the top with the *E* at the end? We always add the *E* for our employees. Whoever had this sticker worked for us."

Skye took the sippy cup from her daughter. "Or still does."

"Possibly, but the color of the logo is different than this year's. If they still worked for us, they should have an updated sticker."

"What about the number? Can you pull up the employee assigned to that number?"

"Sure." Bryn clicked a couple of keys on her laptop. "Looks like the sticker was assigned to a Kiam McClure, who lost his job as a stable hand after several absences. We have a strict punctuality policy due to the nature of our center. We can't have customers unhappy due to lack of staffing."

Jake jotted down the name she provided. "One more question. Who oversees the stable hands? Maybe they would recognize the photo and could tell us more about Kiam."

Bryn stood. "That would be my husband. He's in the VIP section getting ready to compete. I'll drive you over."

"Drive?"

Bryn grabbed her keys and headed for the door. "We use golf carts to get from one end of the center to the other. This place is huge if you haven't noticed."

After an elevator ride down to the ground floor, Bryn led them to a back alcove, where the battery-operated vehicles were stored. They hopped inside and Bryn pulled onto the main thoroughfare, weaving through the crowds.

Vaulted ceilings extended high above their heads with wooden beams decorating the roofline. Every inch of the place reeked of money. Several restaurant options, with a variety of menus from Italian to diner food, filled the space. They even passed by a general store, where Romi spotted a stuffed horse in the window.

"Pony, Mommy, Pony." She pointed.

"I see it."

"Can I have it?"

Bryn slowed the cart to a stop. "I don't mind, if you want to go look."

"We're good. I don't want to hold up the meeting," Skye said.

Jake leaned forward from the back seat. "I'll run in really quick." He jumped out and reached for Romi's hand. "You want to go?"

She hopped out of the cart without any hesitation, and they all entered the shop.

Inside, people meandered, buying a variety of

T-shirts, books, candy, and any gift shop treasure one's heart desired.

Jake moved to the window and let Romi grab the pony, then walked her toward the checkout. He reached for his wallet, but Bryn stopped him. "It's on the house."

"I can pay. I don't mind."

"I insist." Bryn motioned to the cashier. "Skye's my friend, and if this brings her little girl comfort in the midst of everything going on in their lives, then the least thing I'm worried about is a few bucks for a stuffed toy."

Romi ran to her mom. "Look at my pony."

"What do you say?"

"Thank you, Mr. Jake and Ms. Bryn. I'm gonna call him Max."

Someone bumped into Jake from behind, and he stepped out of the aisle. Any massive group of people unnerved him, and he scanned the crowd for potential threats, then motioned toward the exit. "As much as I'm enjoying the moment, we need to move this to a less congested area, if you don't mind."

They returned to the cart, then Bryn drove through a back door and into another corridor. "This is the private VIP hallway for the competitors. I'll take you to what we call the green room. My husband, Walter, should be there."

They wound through a maze of quiet hallways until Bryn punched in a code and opened the door to the large room with green carpet. Tables of refreshments lined two walls, and large-screen TVs hung around the room so the riders could watch the competition unfold in real time.

Bryn scanned the space and then led them to a back sofa tucked into an alcove. Her husband stood when they approached.

"Walter, this is Detective Jake Reed and you remember, Skye Anderson, my childhood friend. They have a few questions about a past employee."

Jake showed him his badge and shook the man's hand. "Thanks for talking with us."

"What can we do for you, Detective?"

Jake pulled the photo up on his phone. "I was wondering if you remember this man, a Kiam McClure. According to your wife, he worked under you as a stable hand."

"Yeah. I recognize him, but we let him go. He no longer works for us."

"How come?"

The man glanced at the television and clenched his fist when another rider made a mistake and had points deducted. "Too many absences."

"Do you remember if he had a skull tattoo, like this one, on his forearm?"

The man broke his gaze from the TV and glanced at the photo. "Not that I ever saw."

Bryn placed a hand on her husband's shoulder. "Walter, we're recording our riders. You can watch them later when Detective Reed isn't here."

"Sorry." The man stepped away from the monitors and motioned to a quieter corner near a snack table. He filled up a small plate with watermelon and a few almonds. "I get so caught up in the people we train, I have a hard time focusing on anything but their rides. Now, what were you asking, Detective?"

"The tattoo? Did Kiam have this on his arm?"

"I never saw any tattoos on the kid. As long as our employees keep them covered, we don't have a policy against them."

"Do you recognize the design?"

Walter popped an almond into his mouth and studied the image again. "I've never seen that specific design before. Skull tattoos are pretty common, but I think I'd remember that if I saw one on him."

"When did you hire Kiam?"

"A couple of summers ago. He was a college kid and possessed exceptional skills with the horses. Every day, he impressed me. I even moved him up to a team lead."

"So, he was a good employee?"

"I didn't have any problems until one day Dante Carello waltzed through the door with Kiam by his side and wanted to invest in our business. I refused."

Jake jotted the news into his phone. The connection between Kiam and Dante proved he was on the right track. "What did Dante do after that?"

"He handed me his business card and told me to call him if anything changed."

"Did you?"

Walter's jaw tensed. "Of course not. Bryn and I don't want anything to do with the man."

"Did you get any retaliation for your dismissal or refusing to work with them?"

"They wanted me to donate to one of their charities. So I did. They left us alone."

After years of investigating the Carello cartel, Jake knew anyone who turned down a business opportunity with Dante ended up at the bottom of a river. Walter's donation probably had saved his family's lives.

"His charity?"

"Yeah. Something about kids."

Walter dug through his wallet, found a card, and handed it to Jake. "Hope's Kids. It's supposed to help inner-city children." A young man approached and leaned toward Walter's ear, then stepped away. "I'm up to compete next. Do you mind if we talk later?"

Jake stepped out of the man's way. "If you think of anything else, let me know."

"Will do." Walter turned and walked out the arena door.

Bryn's gaze followed her husband. "I'm so sorry. He takes his competitions seriously."

"I understand." Jake handed her a business card. "I appreciate your cooperation. If you think of or need anything, call me." He turned to Skye. "You ready?"

She nodded and hugged Bryn. "So good to see you again. Let's really try to get Oscar and Romi together for a playdate."

"I can do you one better. Since Romi loves horses so much, why don't you bring her to our toddler riding class? Oscar loves it. We put them on miniature ponies and start teaching them the basics."

"She'd love that, but we're going to be staying at the Moore Family Ranch and won't be able to make any trips out for a while. But thank you for the offer."

"No worries. I can bring a couple of ponies over and let them ride there. I'll call you after I glance at my schedule."

"Thank you so much. Romi, would you like to ride on a pony?"

"Really?" The little girl reached for Jake. "Can I have a pony ride now?"

"Absolutely." He lifted her to his shoulders. "Hold on tight."

Romi squealed and clasped a free hand onto his head. A fierce protectiveness surged through Jake. The little girl might not be his blood, but he'd make sure no one ever hurt Randy's family again.

* * *

Skye opened the back passenger door so Romi, still clinging to the stuffed horse Jake gave her, could climb into her booster seat. The gift reminded Skye of the bunny her daughter used to carry until the night Randy died. They'd never retrieved Romi's favorite keepsake from her father after the wreck.

She closed the door and squeezed Jake's hand. "Thank you."

"For what?"

"For giving her the stuffed horse. She hasn't had a favorite toy since we lost Boppi in the crash."

"Every kid needs a stuffed animal."

"True, and Romi has plenty of them piled in the corner of her room, but none of them stuck like her favorite rabbit—until now."

"Well, I hope Max brings her some comfort and joy."

Skye loved the sweet side of Jake. He noticed the little details in a person's life, making dreams come true. "I remember this cute teddy bear I had when I was little, called Mr. Muffy. My dad gave him to me for Christmas one year, and I never went to sleep without him."

The corners of Jake's lips curled into a teasing smile. "Even now?"

"Now Mr. Muffy lives in a pretty treasure box inside my closet. I tried to give him to Romi one time, but she never took an interest. What about you? What was your favorite toy?"

The expression on Jake's face hardened. He pulled his hand from hers and opened the passenger door. "I think it's time to get going."

She slipped into her seat and ran her question back through her mind, trying to figure out what she had said wrong. Jake climbed in behind the wheel.

"I'm sorry. I didn't mean to upset you."

He slid the key into the ignition, and the engine roared to life. Cool air from the vent blew into her face. She reached forward and turned the slats down.

Jake shifted the gear into Reverse. "You didn't, but when I was a kid, I didn't have a favorite toy."

"Surely there was something you loved."

He kept his foot on the brake. "I learned at an early age not to get too attached to anything in my house."

Maybe she shouldn't push, but his words raised her curiosity. "What do you mean?"

He let the car roll backward. "When I was around eight years old, I begged my mom for an action hero. Randy had one, and we planned to float them down Crystal Creek in homemade boats. One night, I left the toy on my bedroom floor and went to sleep. When my father came home in an alcoholic rage, he saw the toy on my floor and started ranting about how I needed to pick up after myself. He grabbed it and threw it in the fireplace. I watched the toy melt."

Jake's voice cracked. He adverted his glassy gaze out the driver's side window for a moment, then faced her, his cheeks wet. "After that night, I never asked my mom for anything else."

Her heart ached for the man sitting next to her, fighting back the pain his father inflicted so many years ago. "I'm so sorry. I didn't realize…"

Her words trailed away, the realization of Jake's past hitting her for the first time. He didn't get attached to anything, including her.

"It's not your fault. I don't like discussing my childhood."

They rode in silence for a few miles, but the memory hung between them and stifled any conversation.

Skye wished she hadn't pushed, but maybe she could change the subject and get his mind off the past. "What do you think about Kiam McClure? Do you think he's Randy's killer?"

He shrugged. "We won't know for sure until we find him. I texted Nate to put out an APB, but if he works for the Carellos, we'll have a hard time getting to him. They'll keep him protected."

His words distracted her from their ride until she noticed the vehicle slowing. She glanced out the window. Hayfields ripe for cutting blew in the breeze and the two-lane road stretched past a familiar intersection. Jake pulled off into the shoulder beside the white wooden cross marking the spot where Randy had died.

"Jake, I told you I wasn't ready to come here."

"I know this is hard, but we have to try to at least see if you can recall the details from the accident."

Her breaths tightened in her chest, and Skye fought back emotions rising to the surface. "I can't do this."

"Yes, you can. You'll never be ready but finding Randy's killer is the only way to keep you and Romi safe." He motioned toward her daughter, who was sleeping in the back seat. "Please Skye. Walk me through everything from the night of the crash."

She stared at the intersection. Dark memories flashed through her mind. "But Bryn gave you Kiam's name. The sticker was assigned to him. His truck was there the night Randy was killed. What more do you need?"

"And what if he's not our guy? Then we're back to square one. We have to keep working and putting together as much evidence as possible to hand the district attorney an ironclad case. The defense attorney will bring in ten other men with the same tattoo as Kiam. You have to be the one to identify him."

"I can't—"

"Momma, can I play horsey on the floor?"

Skye stopped midsentence, wiped her cheeks,

and forced a smile to her face before turning towards her daughter. She didn't want Romi to recognize where they were. "I thought you were asleep, baby girl."

"I woke up. Can I play horsey?"

Romi held up her new toy and trotted him across an imaginary path in the air. Skye unbuckled her daughter. If she was playing in the floor, then she wouldn't see their location. Romi hopped her horse across the back seat and made whinnying noises.

"I'll be right back, sweetie."

Skye and Jake stepped from the car after rolling down a couple of windows. He leaned against the fender, dressed in a T-shirt and jeans, his dark brown hair blowing in the cooler evening breeze.

Honeysuckle and fresh-cut grass permeated the air and she tried to relax. Reddish tones streaked across the sunset sky, sure to delight sailors, but this place gave Skye chills.

She closed her eyes and walked to the middle of the intersection. The road was deserted, just like the night of the accident. She placed herself back in the car with Randy beside her, the children's song playing through the radio speakers. Rain spattered the windshield and tall grass bent underneath the weight of the storm. Randy gripped the steering wheel and complained about driving in the rain. She coaxed him into singing the song with them. Randy took her hand in his and kissed her knuckles.

"Have I told you today how much I love you?"

"Not today but get us home in one piece and I'll be grateful."

Randy's smile broadened, and he kissed her hand again. "I can do—"

"Skye!"

Her eyes shot open when Jake yelled. He took a long stride toward the back of the car, his gaze fixed down the road.

A rumble roared to her left. Jake broke into a run, and his gaze shifted. His hands waved for her to move. She followed his previous line of sight. Two motorcycles raced toward her, the riders holding guns raised. Jake pulled his weapon from his holster and aimed. "Get down."

Her heart raced, breaths tightened. She dove for a deep culvert.

Fire pierced the outside of her leg. Skye grabbed above the wound and landed. Jake flung his body on top of hers while bullets sprayed across them. The motorcycles raced by.

"Stay down. Don't move."

Romi.

Her daughter was in the car—alone.

EIGHT

Wet mud seeped through the fabric of Skye's shirt and dampened her jeans, torn where the bullet had grazed her thigh. The deep culvert blocked her vision to the road. She tried to move underneath the weight of Jake's body, but he held her to the ground.

"The shooters might come back. Stay down."

"I have to get to Romi."

"She's on the floorboard of the car with her horse. When I yelled 'get down,' she did exactly what I said. They didn't shoot at the car. Let me make sure the way is clear."

Jake peered at the road, keeping his gun out front, then climbed to the top of the ditch. Skye peeked at the car. The metal doors remained smooth. All the windows were intact and still lowered halfway. Her daughter was nowhere in sight. Jake returned to the ditch and held out his hand.

"They're gone. Let's get out of here before they come back."

Skye stood, the pain in her left outer thigh piercing through her fading adrenaline rush. She swayed, and black dots arrowed through the corners of her vision. His arm wrapped around her waist. "I've got you."

She leaned into him and hobbled across the road, keeping her eyes on the car. The top of Romi's booster seat was visible. Jake opened the back door. Her daughter remained curled on the floorboard hugging her stuffed horse.

Skye lowered herself to the back seat, pulled her daughter into her arms and kissed the top of her head. "You're okay, baby."

"I played hide-and-seek, Momma. Mr. Jake said to get down."

Skye met Jake's gaze and squeezed her daughter tighter. "You did good."

He knelt down and inspected the wound on Skye's outer thigh. "Looks like a graze, but we need to get you back to the ranch and cleaned up."

"Are you hurt, Momma?"

"I'm okay, sweet girl. Just need a Band-Aid. Climb back into your car seat and let's go home. Ms. Carli will want to see your new horse."

Jake closed the back door once Skye had pulled herself inside and propped her injured leg across the console, keeping it elevated.

She should've stayed at the ranch and kept Romi safe instead of venturing out to follow leads. Jake was the detective, not her. She was a post office supervisor and had no place going to the equestrian center to find the man behind the sticker in her memories, especially with her daughter in tow.

Gravel crunched underneath the car's wheels as they pulled into the entrance of the ranch. They parked in front of the guesthouse, and when the car stopped, Skye unbuckled Romi from her seat.

Jake opened the door and helped her from the car, then she leaned against him. "Take me to the porch and grab a couple of towels. We can clean the injury out here, so I don't mess up the inside of the home."

Carli pulled up on a side-by-side outdoor vehicle. "I came as soon as I heard. Zain called and told me what happened. I brought a first aid kit." She rushed to Skye's side. "How are you feeling?"

"I'm fine. It's a graze but burns when I walk. Jake, will you take Romi inside and get her something to drink? I don't really want her to see this."

"Let's go get your thirsty horse some water, Romi."

"Max would rather have a juice box."

Skye smiled as her daughter's continued babble faded when Jake walked her inside. Skye lowered herself to the patio chair and let Carli inspect the wound. Her friend opened the kit and took out some betadine swabs. "It's not deep, but the area on your leg is red. I'll add some antibiotic ointment to help speed up healing. If the area worsens, then you need to see Dr. Frye."

The cleaner was cold and stung. "Candyce and I are on a first-name basis lately. She's been coming by and helping me remember the details surrounding Randy's accident. I'll have her take a look when she's here."

"Has talking to her helped?"

"It has. I was resistant at first, but she's pretty good at listening and helping me focus in on areas my mind tends to ignore."

Carli motioned toward the window. "Would you look at those two?"

Skye turned around and watched Jake squeeze the juice box and squirt liquid into Romi's open mouth. Every time her daughter caught the stream, she broke into giggles.

"I hope she's not getting too attached. Jake's not the kind of man to stay long term."

"Life has a funny way of changing people's minds as we get older. Don't give up on him too quickly. I think God's working on his heart."

"There's nothing between us to give up. We have different goals in life. His focus is work, and he's been clear he doesn't want a family. Our two lifestyles are incompatible."

"Oh, I think y'all are more compatible than

you think, and the chemistry between the two of you is palpable. He cares about you. I can see it in his eyes."

Skye tossed a wadded-up bandage wrapper at her friend. "You read too many romance novels. If Jake Reed cared about me, then he would've stayed the first time around. Besides, Jake's not the commitment type, and I need someone who will be a constant fixture in Romi's life. She's had enough loss to work through for years to come. We both need someone fun and who exudes joy. Jake's too serious and doesn't know how to raise a kid."

Carli fastened the bandage in place and nodded toward the window. "I'm not so sure about that."

Skye turned again. Romi clung to Jake's back as he crawled around on all fours in the living room, making horse sounds. Her daughter giggled and stuck to his T-shirt like a burr. She had never seen Jake so relaxed with any child, much less her own.

Jake toppled over to the side, catching Romi and rolling her onto the floor as she burst into giggles. "You've worn this horsey out."

She hopped back to her feet. "Again, again."

"Horsey needs a water break." Jake stood, grabbed his bottled water from the counter and handed her the sippy cup he filled with a second juice box. She tipped up the cup, drank and then found a book she brought to him. "Will you read this to me?"

"You want to read a book?"

Romi nodded.

He picked up the little girl and hoisted her onto the couch, flipping open the front cover. They followed barn animals down a path and through the woods until they came to a creek to go swimming on a hot summer's day. Romi touched each animal with her fingertip and made the appropriate sound. When they came to the end, he closed the last cardboard page.

"Read it again, Daddy." Romi opened to the front cover and pointed to the cow. "Moo."

Jake stilled for a moment, absorbing the name the little girl had used. He wasn't her father, Randy was.

"Are y'all having fun?" Skye limped in with her leg wrapped in a bandage.

"Will you read the book, Mommy?" Romi said, the name sounding as easy on her lips as the one she'd called Jake. He stood and gave Skye his couch position beside her daughter, still reeling from being called "Daddy."

Skye spread her fingers across the cover of the book. "She hasn't wanted to read much since… well, in a long time."

"Randy used to read to her?"

"Every night. She'd fall asleep in his arms."

Jake looked at the clock. Eight p.m. Most kids went to bed at this time. He backed from the room. "I've got some files to go over and reports to type up. I'll be out on the sunporch if you need me."

Skye turned and faced him. "You hungry? I was thinking of ordering a pizza after I put her to bed."

"I'm good. Nate's bringing me something so we can discuss the case. You need to get some rest. Keep your leg elevated."

He stepped onto the porch, closed the door behind him and exhaled. Romi was only four. She didn't realize what she was saying. Truth was, she missed her father, and reading to her tonight brought back his memory. He'd have to be more careful in the future so she didn't get too attached to him being around.

Nate tapped on the back screen door and entered. "This a bad time?"

"Not at all. Come on in. We've got work to do."

"Speaking of work, I called Natalie and asked her to take a look at Randy's medical report. Did you run our plan by Skye? I figured she'd be joining us so we could go over the details."

"Not yet. She's putting Romi to bed."

"How'd today go? Did she remember anything?"

"She got shot in the leg during a drive-by. We

went back to the intersection where Randy was killed. I figured since the road had little traffic, we'd be safe. They must've been following us. A couple of Honda motorcycles. I got a partial plate—HTN."

"Why didn't you call me?"

"I wanted to get her back here to dress her injury. The bullet barely grazed her leg, but still. I found one of the slugs at the scene." Jake held up a plastic baggie with the metal casing inside.

"I'll take it to forensics when I leave, but we've got bigger problems. My friend in Patrol saw Dante Carello in town today. He's staying at his Mills River estate."

The kingpin's presence in the area increased the danger for Skye and Romi. "He'll escalate the efforts to silence her."

"Of course he will. He doesn't want her tying the Carello cartel to a cop's murder."

"What are you two discussing?" Skye stepped into the enclosed area with a baby monitor in her hand. Sully stayed close to her heels. "And where's the food?"

Nate smacked his leg. "I forgot to stop by Heather's Coffeehouse and get our sandwiches." He pulled out his phone. "I'll call her right now and run back there."

"Don't bother. I ordered enough pizza for us all. The delivery should be here in about fifteen minutes. That gives you enough time to fill me in," Skye said.

Jake brought her up to speed. "Dante Carello's in town."

"Here in Crystal Creek?"

"He has an estate in Mills River, and my guess is he's here for the microchip. When his thugs didn't deliver, he decided to oversee the operation."

Skye took a seat on the couch. "What was on the chip, anyway?"

With a few keys on his laptop, Jake turned the screen for her and Nate to view. "It looks like some kind of schematics and floor plans. Do they look familiar to you?"

Skye leaned forward and scrolled through the images. "Those are blueprints of several of the local post office branches, including mine."

"Post office branches? Why would Randy be looking into those?" Jake asked.

"And these are the routes that my drivers run every day."

Jake studied the documents. "Are you sure?"

"Absolutely. I've memorized everyone's routes because I have to make sure they stay on task and not take any detours. We have GPS trackers in their scanners that tell us where the drivers are at all times."

Jake pulled up another browser window with a map of the area and marked the Carellos' known businesses with red digital pins. "Well, look at that. The cartel's businesses intersect with the postal routes. Randy figured out how Dante transported his product across town without being detected."

Nate pointed at Skye. "Your husband was one smart detective. I don't think I've ever stopped a USPS truck for even a speeding ticket. Have to admit, Dante might be a criminal, but this is brilliant."

"Yeah, but how's he getting the packages onto the trucks without the drugs being detected?" Jake asked.

Gravel crunched in the driveway. The pizza guy arrived and stepped from his car. Skye clambered to her feet.

"I'll get the pizza." Jake stood and moved to the door. "You need to rest your leg." Without waiting for Skye to respond, he stepped off the porch, grabbed for his wallet and looked at the driver. "Hey, man. How much do I owe you?"

"Already been paid for when ordered."

"Great." Jake pushed his wallet back into his pocket, taking in the guy's appearance. His uniform cap hung low over his eyes, and a long-sleeve shirt covered his torso and arms while remaining untucked over khaki shorts.

July temperatures cooled in the evenings, but not enough to wear long sleeves. Jake tried to get a better view of his face. "Aren't you hot?"

The man kept his head down. "Can't stand the mosquitoes biting me at night. Did you order two large pepperoni with mushrooms?"

Still jumpy from the shooting earlier, Jake kept a hand near his weapon as the guy opened the soft-sided container and handed Jake two boxes.

"Yeah, thanks."

The delivery guy tucked the container under his arm and headed back to his car. "Have a good night."

Jake noted the style of car, the license plate tag, and a small Salt Life sticker in the back window, then returned to their meeting. He flipped open the lid of the first pizza box, filling the room with scents of garlic and marinara sauce. He placed the box on the coffee table for everyone to grab their own piece.

Sully nudged at his arm. Skye shooed him away, then lifted a piece of pizza to her plate, but her dog bumped her hand with his nose and whined. She dropped the piece against her shirt.

"Silly dog. What did ya do that for?"

Sully stood and paced between Jake and Nate, continuing to whine, while Skye moved to the kitchen to clean up with a paper towel. The dog kept pushing against their arms every time they reached for a piece.

"Did you not feed this dog today, Skye?" Nate asked.

"This morning, as always. He ate every bite

of his dog food. I'm not sure what his problem is tonight."

Nate stood and lifted a piece to his mouth, but Jake held up his hand. "Wait, don't eat the pizza." He placed a slice on his plate and put the food on the ground in front of Sully. The dog immediately sat and barked. He didn't even try to eat Jake's piece. "Is this Randy's dog? The one he adopted from the department?"

Skye walked back in the room, still wiping at the marinara sauce staining her shirt. "Yeah, why?"

"Go wash your hands and change shirts. Sully's a trained drug dog. The pizza may be laced with something. Most drug dogs sniff out opioid products, particularly fentanyl."

"You mean you think the pizza is drugged?" Skye asked.

Nate grabbed his bag. "I've got a field test kit. Let me swipe the box."

"I'm guessing it's fentanyl because the Carellos are known to traffic it," Jake said, hoping fingerprints were left on the smooth cardboard for them to lift.

With a quick swab inside, Nate inserted the tips back into the appropriate chambers and snapped each column to activate the reaction. After one strong shake, he plunged the swabs into the viewing window and then lined up the

QR code with the app on his phone. "Positive for fentanyl."

Jake donned a pair of gloves, pressed the lid closed, and slid the entire box into a large evidence bag. "Let's take it to the crime lab. Maybe they can pull prints and we can figure out the driver's identity. My guess is he works for Carello."

Skye's eyes widened as she returned to the porch. "But how did they know I ordered a pizza? I called the same place I always do." She pulled her cell from her pocket.

"They must've hacked your phone." Jake reached for her device. "Have you downloaded any new apps lately, clicked on any text links or used open-source internet?"

"At the library, I used public Wi-Fi."

"We'll need to do a factory reset which will wipe everything clean. They probably hacked your phone through the library's network. Are your photos, history, any documents or notes backed up?"

"Everything's on my Google Drive."

Jake tapped the reset button. "Even after this, let's still get our cybersecurity guy to run some tests and make sure the phone is clean. Also, let's do a sweep of the house for any listening devices."

"I'll schedule a team to come out," Nate said.

"Did you get a look at the delivery guy's face when you went out to get the pizza?"

"Not enough. His hat was pulled low, and it was getting dark. If he works for Carello, then that would explain his long-sleeve shirt. He wanted to hide his tattoo."

Nate tapped through a few screens on his phone. "Good thing Zain has cameras mounted all around this house. Let's see if we can get a better view of our guy." He scrolled through a couple of camera displays. "Not that angle, not that angle. There. A straight shot."

Nate passed his phone to Jake, and he zoomed up the display. "He doesn't just work for the Carellos. This guy used to work for Walter Cavanaugh. Our pizza boy is Kiam McClure."

NINE

Morning sun and the wakeup call of birds roused Jake from his slumber on the couch. The older piece of furniture didn't sleep like his bed, but despite the late working hour and lack of a pillowtop mattress, Jake's body didn't ache. He propped up on one arm and glanced at his watch. Six o'clock in the morning. His daytime replacement should arrive in thirty minutes.

Nate had left around midnight to take the opioid-laced pizza and bullet casings to the lab for testing. Jake and Skye had stayed up until 1:00 a.m. searching for the partial plate on the bike with no match.

Instead, they'd moved on to reviewing post office employees from Skye's work laptop. She'd pulled up all the human resource files, but no connection between Randy's files and her colleagues surfaced.

He yawned, shuffled into the kitchen, and made some coffee, then returned to the porch with a mug to look over the images still displayed on the monitor.

Footsteps shuffled behind him. "What do you think?"

Jake turned at Skye's voice, and she took a seat beside him with a cup in her hand, her hair pulled into a ponytail and face makeup-free. The morning light revealed even more of her natural beauty and highlighted her green eyes.

He tapped Penny Shaw's photo and studied the woman's red hair and pale skin. "Tell me about her again."

"There's not much to tell. She's single with a long-time boyfriend and has worked underneath me for seven years now. She's punctual, finishes her deliveries on time and doesn't complain. She's one of my best workers and friends. Penny and I grew up together. Trust me, she's not involved in this."

"Sounds like a model employee."

"Except she doesn't like our postmaster, Cale Hudson. According to her, he'll step on the little guy to succeed."

"Did he step on her?"

"Apparently. She applied for his position and didn't get chosen because he pulled in a few favors with regional leadership and got the job even though he had less experience."

"Does she have any financial troubles?"

"Not that I know of."

"What about Cale? Any reason he would distribute drugs using the post office vehicles?"

"I still find it hard to believe the Carellos can get drugs onto our trucks with the amount of security at our distribution centers. They have them locked down with all kinds of X-ray equipment and drug-sniffing dogs. They monitor everything going in and out of that facility. Plus, every package is X-rayed and tracked before being shipped to the regional branches."

Jake pulled the routes up from Randy's file. "Your husband thought different. He figured out the drugs were being transported on the delivery trucks. Tell me how your trucks are loaded."

"Large trucks roll in from the distribution centers with our packages every morning. They are unloaded and moved to our trucks. Every package has a bar code, and every postal worker carries a GPS scanner. Like I said before, all of our movements are tracked, so we can't run off on errands or take long breaks without leadership knowing. That's part of my job, to make sure our employees deliver the packages in a timely manner and no one gets off course."

"Tell me about Cale. Do you have a photo of him?"

"Not in human resources, but he has a social media profile I can pull up for you."

Skye typed in the address and clicked on a link. "As far as I know, he doesn't have money issues. He makes a wad working as the postmaster for our area, but he did hire two new guys as delivery drivers, Chad Wyndel and Thomas Helbing. I trained Thomas, but Chad came on board after my incident."

"What were they like?"

"Penny trained Chad and said he seems like a nice guy. Thomas is harmless. A super-quiet guy who keeps to himself and gets his work done. However, they both drive trucks through the two areas in the city most known for drug activity. We always tell them to be careful not to get shot."

She clicked on a couple of screens. "Here's a photo of Thomas. Let me see if there's one of Chad. I haven't even had a chance to look at any files on him."

Jake's phone rang from a number at the Charlotte Police Department's office. "I need to take this."

Skye nodded, and he stepped into the kitchen. "Detective Reed here."

"Howdy, stranger. I don't suppose you're back in Charlotte, are ya?"

Sergeant Todd Butler had supervised Jake in his first detective's job when he moved to the big city.

"Well, hey man. Good to hear from you and I'm in Crystal Creek. Why? What's up?"

"I need to talk to you about a case. We've got a big one—drugs are crossing three counties.

Pounds of fentanyl, heroin and oxy. I was hoping to entice you to come back this way and help us work this. There's a promotion in it for you."

"You want me to quit my job here and come back to Charlotte? I can't do that, Todd. I've got my mom to consider. She needs me here."

"I understand, but you're the expert on the Carello cartel. These trafficking incidents and murders are linked to them."

"So is the case I'm working on here. We've tracked shipments as far as Rutherford County."

"Ours extends to Cleveland. We may be looking at the same operation but from different sides. Do you think you can come down here for a debriefing and compare notes?"

"Not a problem. I'll have to look at my schedule and see when I can get away."

"Great. Let me know."

Jake ended the call and returned to the sunroom where Skye studied the photos.

"You need to take a look at this." She stepped back and turned the computer screen for him to view. "Chad Wyndel is our pizza guy."

"Wait, what? How can that be? I thought our pizza guy is Kiam McClure. Isn't that what we decided last night?"

She dug her fingertips into her long hair and exhaled, still staring at the screen. "Looks like Chad Wyndel and Kiam McClure are one and the same."

He took a seat and compared the images. Either the two men were identical twins or this was one twist he didn't see coming. "Then it's time to bring him in."

"If you can find him. I texted Penny and Chad has been absent for the past three days. I don't suppose the person who called you a few minutes ago might be able to help us find this man's location."

"Maybe." Jake's replacement guard pulled into the driveway. "My former sergeant in Charlotte has quite a few connections."

"I didn't realize y'all kept in touch."

"We still talk sometimes, but he thinks there may be a connection between a case they're working on in Charlotte and our Carello friends here."

He left out the part about the job promotion. He'd made Randy a promise he planned to keep—to finish the case and make sure Skye and Romi were safe. Then if Jake needed a change, and if his sergeant held the position for him, he could consider the offer.

Sully plodded into the room and nudged his hand with his cold, wet nose. Jake squatted down and rubbed the dog's neck. "You did a good job last night, buddy. You kept us from eating the pizza."

"I don't even want to think about the outcome had Sully not been here."

Jake glanced back at the photo of their suspect. "I'll check with Nate and see if we got any prints off the box. We'll call the pizza place, too, and get a list of employees."

"Did Nate find out if the pizza was laced?"

He hated to share more bad news, but after receiving his partner's text early this morning, he had to tell her. "Lab results came back and confirmed the food was laced with a lethal dose of fentanyl. One bite and we all would've died."

Skye dug her trembling hands into Sully's fur. "That's so messed up."

"We're going to get him. I promise. I'm not going to let him hurt you or Romi."

The reality darkened her gaze. "What if we don't? They'll keep coming, and you've never been a small-town kind of guy. You can't protect me forever. There are too many opportunities for you to succeed. It may be best if Romi and I pack up and head to another part of the country. Far enough away so the Carello cartel will forget we ever existed."

"You can't leave. You have to help us identify Randy's killer."

"Not if it means putting my daughter's life at risk."

Jake understood the stress of her position and didn't blame her for wanting to disappear. The emotional drain of being hunted and stalked with the threat of death took an emotional toll on even the strongest of victims, but he had a job to do, and his priority was finding the man who killed his best friend—with or without her.

Skye climbed the stairs to Romi's room, still processing the information Randy had collected on her employer. The depth of her husband's investigation filled her with fear for her daughter. The postal service reached every part of their nation, and if Dante Carello had found a way to infiltrate their base network and bypass the distribution centers, then his reach was limitless.

Before opening the files, she contemplated a move, somewhere far away, where no one in Crystal Creek would think to look, not even Jake. Out West, maybe. Randy had always wanted to spend more time in Montana. But if the information Randy had assembled proved true, even if she ran, well, she and Romi would always be looking over their shoulders.

Jake couldn't protect them forever and from the worried look on his face this morning after scrolling through the images, she needed a better plan.

Romi's giggles and words drifted down the hallway to her. As long as she had her daughter, they could live anywhere and be a family. Witness protection offered a new opportunity at life with a secret identity, even if she had to quit her job. Might be a nice time to open her own photography studio like she always wanted. The vast landscapes in Montana provided great scenery for images.

Romi's laughter shrieked with delight, which usually indicated a little girl up to no good. Skye hastened her steps and swung open the bedroom door.

"Mommy, do you want to play with me?" Romi sat in the floor with her post office set and held up one of the cars for Skye to take.

She reached for the toy and glanced at her daughter's bed. "You're up really early this morning."

"I wanted to play post office."

"I see."

Romi pointed to the little yellow plastic building with a blue roof. "You need to deliver your mail, Mommy."

Skye pushed her blue-and-white plastic truck across the carpet. "Load me up, little one."

Romi placed the postal person into the other blue-and-white truck and drove it into the side of the play office, then back out again. She rolled it over to her barn and loaded up a few Lego pieces inside. Skye scooted closer, pointing to the plastic bricks her daughter placed in the toy truck.

"What are those, Romi?"

"Paci-ges."

"Packages?"

Her daughter nodded. Skye glanced at the

Lego block packages, then studied the ones hidden in the toy barn.

With a quick kiss on her daughter's head, she ran to the window overlooking the drive. Jake stood by his car talking on the phone. She rapped on the glass and flung open the window. "I know how they're getting the drugs on the trucks without being detected."

He turned and glanced up at her. "How?"

"They're bypassing the distribution centers, by driving the trucks to legitimate stops on their route and loading up packages from a business next door, then they deliver the goods to their customers. No cop pulls them over. Why would they? They're the postal service."

"I have to stop at the department to interview a suspect, but if you go with me, afterward we'll swing by the branch and follow the drivers en route."

"Let me call Carli to watch Romi and I'll be right down."

She locked the window back in place and swung her daughter around in the air. "We may not have to move to Montana after all."

TEN

Jake entered the interrogation room and scraped a chair across the floor. He tried not to gag from the stale scents of body odor, sweat and loud musk cologne emanating from the suspect's failed attempt to cover his stench. Fluorescent lights hummed overhead, casting the man's face in a pale, sickly glow while his hands trembled, indicating withdrawal symptoms from his most recent high.

Jake popped a strong piece of spearmint gum into his mouth, hoping the whiff he inhaled might overshadow the foulness of the room.

Nate leaned back in his chair next to him and eyed the low-level drug addict seated across the table. His partner embodied the bad cop persona with ease, freeing Jake to focus on collecting the obscure facts in the case.

Dropping a folder onto the table, Jake flipped open the cover. "Sudz Miller. Two counts of felony possession with intent to distribute, and this isn't the first time you've been charged. We've got multiple counts of possession, trafficking and two counts of assault with a deadly weapon. You did a five-year stint in prison already, and today you were arrested by one of our undercover cops for selling heroin. Why don't we start there?"

Their suspect couldn't be more than twenty years old, tall, lanky, and his grungy hair needed a serious shampooing. "The drugs weren't mine."

Nate dropped his tilted chair to the floor with a bang. "That's what all addicts say when they get arrested. Nothing but lame excuses. I can see the needle tracks in your arms and your heroin-constricted pupils. Why don't you try again?"

Sudz kept his head down, and Jake slid a photo across the table. "We have you on video selling drugs to one of our undercover cops. Here's a photo of the sale. We also know someone supplied you with the stash. Wanna tell me where you got the drugs?"

The kid shrugged. "Just had it."

"You weren't dealing to pay off your debt to the Carellos?"

"Never heard of 'em."

Jake stood to put some distance between him and the junkie, but the smell didn't seem to fade. "Come on, Sudz. We know you work at one of their warehouses filled to the brim with various opioids. The place is like an addict's dream world. I bet you didn't think they'd miss a few little baggies if you took some and sold them to make extra cash."

"Man, I told you. I don't work for Carello."

Jake strode across the room and retrieved another photo, tossing on the table the image of Sudz working at the warehouse. "I think you do. We have street cam footage of you loading postal trucks at one of their facilities."

Sudz glanced at the picture.

"Why don't you give me the addresses of the other warehouses Carello owns and maybe I'll put in a good word with the district attorney."

Sudz dropped his head and didn't respond. Nate picked up the conversation. "Or you can keep thinking you're smarter than us and head to a low-security prison, where the Carellos have plenty of paid thugs who take care of rats who talk to the cops. Not to mention what they'll do when they find out you were skimming off the top without permission?"

Jake forced a straight face at his partner's addendum. Nate was good. They played off each other to paint a masterpiece of the suspect's future should he choose not to cooperate.

Sudz wouldn't last a minute with criminals hardened by years of confinement. Carello had men on the inside who took care of snitches. "You help us, Sudz, and we help you. It's that easy."

The kid pushed back the hood of his shirt. "It's not that easy. They'll kill me if I talk."

"They'll kill you if you don't," Nate said.

Jake slid a pad of paper across the table. "You think that by not talking, the Carellos are going to let you live? Everyone knows if you get caught, interrogated by the police and then released, Dante puts a hit out on your head, no questions asked."

"He's right. The only option you have is to tell us what you know, then we can talk to the district attorney and some of our other connections to secure a prison far away, where the Carellos will forget all about you. If not, I doubt you'll be alive by morning."

Jake didn't give Sudz time to contemplate an alternative solution. "Write down the addresses of the warehouse and the name of your contact."

Sudz picked up the pen lying next to the pad of paper and listed the addresses. "There's nothing in there but sealed boxes. None of the workers know what's inside."

"My guess is enough fentanyl to kill the population of a small country. Now, what about a name?" Jake asked.

"I don't know his name. We don't ever talk to him or see him. We cut and sell the drugs, then he gets half of the profits."

He let the name slide for now and instead

passed a photo of Skye across the table for the man to review. "Do you know this woman?"

Sudz glanced at the image. "Yeah. I've seen her."

"Where?"

"On the street. I keep an eye out for customers and cops. I help them make connections and warn them if anybody's sniffing around. One of the main guys texted a photo of your girl to me and told me to let them know if I ever saw her."

"And did you?" Nate asked.

"Yeah. She was at the public library the other day. That's in my zone."

"You gave Carello her location?"

"Not Carello. I told you, I don't work for him."

"Then who?"

"I don't know. I do my job and get an envelope of cash in a locker. There's no need for me to know any names. I texted the number they sent me."

Jake tensed with the news, a streak of rage splitting up his spine. This twenty-year-old kid with no future had initiated Skye's attack and alerted a hit man to her whereabouts. She'd been mere seconds from death at the library. "Where's the locker?"

"They send us to a different drop every week. I've never had the same locker twice."

Jake slapped his hand on the table, letting a bit of the rage release into the sting of his palm.

"You didn't give any consideration about what they would do to her if you ratted her out?"

"Hey, man. I'm not a rat."

"Really?" Jake's hands tightened into fists. "Then what do you call telling a hit man the location of an innocent victim? I should arrest you right know for aiding and abetting in an attempted murder."

"Murder? You said you'd reduce my sentence if I talked."

Nate shot Jake a calming look. Time to shut his own mouth before he spooked their only connection.

"How does the operation work, Sudz?" Nate asked. "How do they contact you?"

"It's all done through burners. We change them out every few weeks. New ones are delivered to us, and we destroy the old ones."

Nate jotted a few notes. "What does the guy look like who delivers the phones to you?"

"We get them through the regular mail. My postal lady brings the box to my door every week."

Jake straightened in his chair. "So, your phones are delivered through your mail carrier from the post office?"

"Neither snow, nor rain, nor heat, nor gloom of night stops them from making their deliveries…or something like that."

"And how are you notified when you need to be looking for a specific person?"

"Everyone's put on notice. A photo goes out, and we all keep our eyes open. If we make a spot, then we give notice to a different burner number every day. Everything's anonymous. They don't tell us anything because we're the low men on the totem pole. If we get picked up, then we know nothing."

Jake removed Sudz's burner phone from a plastic baggie and slid the device across the table. "Unlock it."

"Man, why? I've already told you everything I know."

Nate took the suspect's finger in his hand and pressed the tip to the print reader on the back. His phone opened.

"You need a search warrant to look through that."

"Already got one." Nate tapped the message app and slid the phone across to Sudz. "Tell your contact the girl he wants is back in your zone outside the library again."

Sudz typed in the message, showing the screen to Jake and Nate, then hit Send. Jake snatched the device from Sudz's hand and waited for a response. He noted the number and scrolled through the call history. All the outgoing numbers changed. "How do you know the number to text?"

"We have a morning roll call text with new contact information every day."

Jake motioned for Nate to follow him from the room.

"Tell the DA to reduce my jail time since I'm cooperating," Sudz said.

The door slammed closed behind them.

"Randy's files stated a connection to the post office, and he thought they were distributing the drugs through the facilities but never had the proof to back up his theory. Now we have a member of the cartel who's caught red-handed confirming their involvement. I'm going to have to call the Office of the Inspector General."

"With what?" Nate asked. "We don't have proof the Carellos trafficked drugs through the post office or their distribution centers. Those facilities use top-notch security cameras and dogs to sniff the packages. All we have are a few cell phones being delivered to their network, and the last time I checked, that's not illegal."

"Skye's with me. She figured out they're bypassing the distribution centers, understands their working protocols, and knows the staff. Maybe she can provide some insight."

Nate tossed his empty coffee cup into a trash can. "We need her to head back to work so we can catch whoever's connected there."

"I'm not using her as bait."

"But if we have her covered with cops, she'll

be safe, and we can bring this killer in before he kills again."

Jake racked his brain for another way, another person to go back into the lion's den as a target, but they didn't have anyone who could pose as Skye. She was their only option.

The suspect's burner phone vibrated in his hand. A text message came through for Sudz.

Rats die.

Jake handed the device to Nate. "They know he's with us. They're not going to listen to anything he tells them now or send any more information to this phone."

There went another lead out the door, but Sudz had confirmed the Carello's connection with the post office. Jake doubted the shipments delivered only contained cell phones. Somehow they disguised drugs and placed them on the trucks, but nothing Randy had discussed in his notes gave a clue to their cloaking process.

Jake walked back to his desk, where Skye waited for him. "You ready?"

"Did the runner give you any information?" she asked.

"One of the nearby warehouse addresses, but before we go there, let's head to the post office. I want photos of every driver in their trucks."

He grabbed up a backpack and handed it to her. "Are you any good with a camera?"

Skye hit the shutter button again, snapping several photos of the numbered delivery trucks parked in the loading area of the postal facility. Jake hopped back in the car and handed her a coffee.

"Waffle House was the closest place."

"Thanks." Skye took a sip. The creamed liquid warmed her and provided a jolt of energy. "The big trunk should be here any minute to unload the mail. Then the carriers load their trucks, and usually everyone's en route no later than 10:00 a.m."

"Do you think any of the drugs are loaded on the trucks here?"

"Doubtful. They have to scan all the items placed in their cargo holds, and security cameras catch every angle. They'd get caught."

Jake held a scope to his eye. "Then they must pick up the drugs during their route."

"True but remember they can't venture off their route. We track them. Leadership wants to make sure the carriers deliver the mail in a timely fashion and don't stop for unnecessary breaks or go shopping."

"How many carriers are there?"

"About twenty, but every facility is different."

"Then whoever is working with the cartel has

to have a legitimate business pick up next to one of the Carellos' warehouses."

"I have all the postal routes on my laptop." She unzipped her backpack and pulled out her computer. "Let's cross-reference those again with the Carellos' real estate holdings, if you have them."

"I've got them all listed."

"Perfect." Skye pulled up the employee routes. "There's a line that runs up Founder's Cove and out to Hook's Creek."

"The Carellos don't have any property there."

"Are you sure?"

Jake zoomed through each of the holdings to double-check. "Positive. What about Chad's routes? Or I guess we should call him Kiam, since we know he is one and the same."

Skye viewed the businesses listed on Jake's page with Kiam's main route. "Nothing at the beginning of his stops but let me keep looking."

"What about the warehouse address Sudz provided? Do they schedule any pickups?"

"Not to that specific location, but the business next door schedules a pickup every day. Looks like they share a loading dock, which makes for an easy grab for both sets of packages without anyone becoming suspicious."

"And who makes those pickups?"

Skye tapped a few keys. "Our friend Kiam McClure, also known as Chad Wyndel."

"Then let's go take a look. Maybe Chad will stop by."

Skye placed a hand on his wrist. "Wait. Look at this. Chad also has another stop at a private airstrip. That would make it easy to distribute drugs anywhere."

"What's the name?"

"Josephson Airfield."

"Never heard of it. Are the owners listed?"

"Mountain Shores Trust owns the property, but I've never heard of them, either."

"There's only one way to find out. We'll stop at the warehouse first, then drive out to the airstrip."

After a fifteen-minute drive, Skye scanned the perimeter while Jake parked across the street from the building. He called for backup, and they waited for Nate and a few other officers to arrive. The lot was empty and the warehouse dark. Jake reached behind her seat and pulled out a long tool.

"What's that?" she asked.

"A sledge to pry the side door open. We've got two cameras, one at each front door, but the side entrance is blind."

Nate pulled in with a few patrol officers in tow. He parked beside them, then rolled down his window. "What have you found?"

Jake pointed at the building. "This is the address of the warehouse Sudz provided, but it wasn't listed in the database for Carello."

"My drivers have pickups located at the business next door." Skye pointed to the dry cleaner. "We think they're picking up Carello's product during the same stop, then transporting to a private airstrip."

"Have you ever heard of Josephson Airfield?" Jake asked his partner.

"Afraid not but using the government's very own trucks to move their product is genius. Pretty smart way to stay under the radar since they figured out a way to bypass the distribution centers."

"They're delivering right under our noses without raising any red flags."

Skye leaned forward. "As long as they don't scan the product and return the truck without any evidence inside, it's an almost flawless plan."

"Who did you say owns the airstrip?" Nate asked.

Jake tapped his computer screen again. "The name is Josephson Airfield, and the property is owned by a Mountain Shores Trust."

"I can run some checks on the history. See who's hands the land passed through over the years."

"Sounds good, but while everyone's here, let's head inside before the postal workers make their run. If they come in while we're there, then we can arrest them."

He turned to Skye. "I would normally tell you to stay in the car, but since they're trying to harm you, stay with me."

Early-morning light filtered through the clouds as they moved closer to the facility.

Skye followed Jake as he rounded the back of the building and led the team to an isolated entrance, steering clear of the two cameras. Skye tried to peer in through a window, but someone had painted them black. Broken glass from a streetlight crunched underneath her shoes.

Jake jiggled the locked door handle and then placed the black sledge into the small space between the door and the frame, busting the barrier wide-open. The team of officers flooded into the space. She remained with Jake, who dropped the tool and retrieved his weapon. "Stay behind me."

She flipped off the safety on her pepper spray, and Jake glanced at the container. "Don't spray me with that stuff, either."

"I'll be careful."

They entered the building. Metal racks rose to the top of ten-foot ceilings, and blue bins filled the shelves. Yellow tape marked the floor around each rack, and chains hung ready to be fastened when moving product from the top. Ten forklift trucks rimmed the back of the facility for workers to maneuver containers onto trucks at the loading docks. The place reminded her of a home improvement store but housed deadly narcotics.

Jake walked to the row closest to them, flipped open the top of one of the bins and beamed his light inside to view the contents. Bags of fentanyl—at least a hundred pounds—filled the container.

"That's enough narcotics to kill millions of people. Fentanyl's fifty times stronger than heroin, and it only takes about three milligrams to end a life."

"No wonder Carello wants me dead. This is massive."

"And this is only one of his warehouses. Imagine if we found them all."

A clang from the other end of the building echoed, and a beam of light filtered across the floor. Skye, Jake, and the team squatted down behind the bins, ready for any resistance.

A curvy, shadowed figure stepped through the door and tossed her red hair from her shoulder. "Are the packages ready?"

A larger man followed her inside. "We've got them right here."

Skye inhaled a quick breath, clasping her hand over her mouth before leaning close to Jake. "I know that voice. That's my friend, Penny. She can't be involved in this."

Jake pulled his weapon. "Stay hidden. I don't want them to see you."

He crept into the shadows of the shelves, moving farther from where Skye stood. She peeked between the bins and kept low. Penny's colleague climbed onto a forklift and maneuvered the machine into a row.

Jake's team members moved with him, sticking to the shadows until he was close. He stepped into view.

"Don't move." His words resounded across the room as he aimed his weapon at Penny. Other officers dressed in black Kevlar and SWAT gear surrounded her. She screamed and raised her hands in the air.

The driver on the fork truck shifted into gear and sped toward Jake. Metal spikes used to lift pallets raised to the level of his chest. The other members shifted their aim.

Skye stepped into the aisle. "Jake!"

He pivoted, fired two rounds and hit the driver with a fatal shot. The fork truck stopped within inches of him. Skye rushed forward, stopping when Penny's gaze landed on her friend.

"Skye? What's going on?" Penny asked.

Jake climbed onto the fork truck and pressed two fingers to the man's neck and shook his head. One of the other officers stepped close to Penny, keeping a gun aimed on her.

Jake moved behind the woman and pulled her arms behind her back, placing handcuffs on her wrists. "Penny Shaw, you're under arrest for the felony possession and distribution of narcotics."

"What? That's absurd. I'm not a part of whatever this is, and I'm certainly not distributing any drugs. Chad was absent today. I'm filling in for him."

"I'll take your statement when we get to the precinct." Jake led Penny past where Skye stood, toward a bench along the side wall.

Penny met her gaze, pleading. "Please, Skye, tell him I'm not a part of this. You know me. We've been friends for years. I've never done drugs."

But Skye didn't say a word. Right now, she wasn't sure if she could trust anyone, especially a friend who might be involved in the murder of her husband.

ELEVEN

Blue lights flashed against the warehouse walls while police officers and crime scene investigators scoured the area. Local camera crews congregated outside the building in the hot noon sun, waiting for Jake and Sergeant Zain Wescott to step in front of their lenses.

Inside the building, the medical examiner inspected the man he'd shot. The lifeless body remained seated on the fork truck. The pointed metal bars hung stationary at chest height. Jake cringed at how close he'd come to being skewered. He hoped Zain agreed with his actions, even though Internal Affairs reviewed all officer-involved shootings. Once his gun discharged, he'd triggered an investigation into his conduct.

Medical examiner Natalie Kensington glanced up at Zain and Jake. "The male victim is Maurice Donahue, known for his ties to the Carello family. The evidence supports Detective Reed's account of events, with two shots fired to the middle of the chest, ending in a fatality. I'll take the body back to the lab so our pathologist can perform a thorough autopsy. If you need me to make a statement, I'm happy to give one in support of Jake and what happened here. From the angle of the shots and the position of the suspect, Jake's blessed not to have been pierced with those blades."

"Thanks, Nat. I appreciate your professional opinion on this." Zain faced Jake. "We still have to follow protocol. I need your weapon, and you need to head to the hospital to get your blood drawn for a toxicology report."

"And what then?"

"Since witnesses corroborated your story, you'll be put on station duty until the shooting board can hold a hearing and clear you to return to the field. Also, protocol requires a psych cval."

"And what about Skye? Am I going to be removed from her guard rotation also?"

"You can't be in the field until you're cleared, so I'll find someone else to take your place." Zain typed out a message on his phone. "I'm guessing this facility belongs to Dante Carello?"

"You know they won't sit back and let one of their operations go down without retaliation, and no other officer on the force knows them like I do. I've worked their cases for years. I know their mode of operation. You can't expect me not to be there for Skye and her daughter."

"If Skye invites you to stay at the ranch as a personal guest, then there's nothing I can say. But Jake, you need to be careful. This incident was clearly self-defense, but if you do anything while you're on leave that piles onto what happened today, I won't be able to stop leadership from coming after you."

"Understood."

The Carello cartel had killed hundreds of people, maybe even thousands, in the name of their business ventures. They never let a strike on their members go without some kind of punishment. When someone killed a member of the Carello team, their name was added to a hit list. Jake was no exception.

Skye stood at the warehouse door, her legs tired from the hours of waiting for the investigation to finish. Her gaze shifted to Penny, who had been moved to the back seat of a running patrol car parked in the shade to avoid the heat of the late-afternoon sun.

They'd been friends for years, and Skye had trusted her with so many secrets and feelings. Some including Jake. Now, she was questioning everything, like the new shoes and designer purses Penny bought, the nice jewelry she always wore and some of the gifts she'd given her friends. The post office paid well, but not enough for Penny to afford the luxuries she often purchased.

The long day ached inside Skye's head, and she craved a hot bath, snuggles with Romi and a good night's sleep in her own bed, but her desires would have to wait.

Her postmaster arrived and approached the scene. He stopped at the squad car.

Jake stepped up to her side. "Who's that?"

"Cale Hudson. He's my and Penny's supervisor. The postmaster I told you about."

The tall man with broad shoulders and dark hair marched toward the warehouse doors. Jake and Skye walked out to meet him.

"What do you think you're doing, Detective? Why are you arresting my postal worker like this? She had nothing to do with whatever is going on here."

Jake put up his hands. "Sir, we're following protocol."

"Following protocol? Penny Shaw was filling in for a colleague who called in sick today. She doesn't need or deserve this."

"Then maybe you can tell us why she was picking up shipments of fentanyl."

Cale's eyes widened at the announcement and he hesitated for a moment. "I had her stand in for Chad. I have to make management decisions every day to make sure our shipments are delivered on time."

"So, Chad regularly picks up shipments of fentanyl?"

He waved a dismissive hand. "That's not what I meant. No one is picking up fentanyl."

"But usually, we call in substitutes when someone's sick instead of pulling others from their normal routes," Skye said.

"Last time the sub filled in, she refused to take their packages because they didn't have the right labels on them. The customers didn't like her asking questions and banned her from their facility. Since Penny ran the route before Chad came onboard, I thought it would be best if they saw a familiar face."

Skye motioned toward the car. "Did you tell her to pick up the packages even if they didn't have the appropriate labels?"

"But they do. I made a special trip down here a few weeks ago and saw the packages myself. The labels were fixed to the boxes and slated for a specific delivery destination. I didn't see anything out of the ordinary," Cale said.

Jake moved back to the door, picked up one of the boxes and handed it to Cale. "Did you scan the bar code while you were here?"

The man took the box from Jake's outstretched hand, barely giving it a glance. "There were no red flags, and I made sure the bar codes worked. We're forbidden to ask what's inside. I don't want to know, anyway. To me a package is just a package."

Jake took out his phone and pulled up an image. "That's where you're wrong." He flashed the screen toward him. "Inside each of those warehouse bins is enough fentanyl to take out an entire town's population, maybe even a region."

Skye waited for the shock to register in Cale's expression, but the expected reaction never came. She straightened. "If Penny's not involved, she'll be released and back to work before you know it."

She'd seen the kind of man Cale was when he didn't get his way. He wasn't aggressive, but he had a way of manipulating the outcome he wanted, no matter the cost. He stepped close to Jake and towered over him by a couple of inches. "This isn't over."

Jake didn't back away but kept his gaze focused. "Not by a long shot."

The man turned and stormed back to his car with his cell phone to his ear. Jake faced her. "He's intense. Do you think he's telling the truth about Penny?"

Skye glanced back to the sedan, where her friend remained. "I don't know what to believe anymore."

"You know, if Nate finds evidence of her involvement, she won't be going home."

"You don't believe him?"

Jake stared at the man. "I'm not sure yet. He didn't seem too surprised about the fentanyl shipments. Makes me wonder if he really did know what was inside those bins and if Penny's in on something with him."

"She's not some hardened criminal out of Charlotte, Jake. I've known her for a lifetime. Penny's never hurt a fly or ever been in trouble. She's one of my best friends."

They walked toward his SUV and Jake opened the passenger door for her. Skye slipped into her seat and grabbed her laptop while he settled in behind the wheel.

She clicked through several screens. "I keep coming back to something. If Penny scanned the bar code on the packages, then they should be in our system. Surely we haven't been shipping boxes of fentanyl without knowing it."

"Even if she scans them, their contents aren't known, correct?"

"Every scanned item has to go through our system. If the packages are scanned and don't arrive, then an investigation is launched. I can't figure out how they are scanning the boxes but bypassing the centers. Do you still have the images of some of the boxes?"

"Yeah."

"Read off one of the numbers beneath the bar code to me."

The digits Jake supplied didn't match any in

the system. Skye searched again. "I don't understand. They should be here if she scanned them."

"Maybe they're dummy codes."

"What do you mean?"

"The shipping labels are printed to look like
the post office labels, but the bar codes direct the
information to another location. If we track the
code to the IP address where the information is
delivered, then we find our Carello connection."

Skye snapped her laptop lid closed. "And Randy's killer."

Jake rolled down both windows in the SUV
and let the cooler evening air circulate inside the
cab, calming the day. His thoughts swirled with
the stakeout, warehouse bust and arrest replaying in his mind. He glanced at Skye who stared
out the window without a word.

"Penny for your thoughts?"

She rolled her eyes at him. "Really?"

"Too soon for a joke?"

"She doesn't deserve to be involved in any of
this. Chad or Kiam, whatever his name is, should
be in a holding cell right now with officers questioning him, not her."

"If she's innocent, then Nate will release her,
but she was caught at the scene of a crime. As
for Kiam, he's on the top of my list. Well, Nate's
list now since I'm on leave."

Skye rested her head against the seat. "With

everything that's happened and the scene at the warehouse this afternoon, I'm ready to get back to the safe house and wrap my arms around Romi. Plus, I'm starving. We missed lunch and dinner."

"I can stop by a fast-food restaurant if you want."

"Thanks, but I've got some leftovers in the fridge. I'll heat those up, then curl up on my couch with my daughter and watch the latest princess movie. I could use a fairy tale right about now."

"I'll pass on the princess movie, but my king-size bed is calling my name. Your sunroom couch has taken a toll on my back, and since I'm on leave, I'm planning to stretch out and sleep late. You really should get something more comfortable out there."

"Hey, talk to Carli. It's her house, not mine. I'm fortunate to have a place to stay that's safe."

"I can say, the couch is better than sleeping in my car."

She laughed and shifted in her seat toward him. "Are you worried about the internal review?"

"Maybe a little, but this isn't my first time."

"You've killed someone on duty before?"

His body tensed at her question. According to Randy's file, he'd never shot anyone. The dangers of working as a detective in a large city warranted different responses. "Dispatch called me to a domestic case. Some of those can be volatile."

"What happened?" she asked in a whisper, almost as if she didn't really want to know.

"My partner and I drove to a small house in downtown Charlotte. We'd been there before several times, but this time was different. The neighbor called and said she heard gunshots. When we busted in, the suspect started shooting. My partner entered through the front entrance, and the suspect shot him in the abdomen with two rounds. I came in from the back, and when the man swung his gun in my direction, I took my shot. He dropped to the floor."

"Did the woman and your partner live?"

"She did and still sends me birthday and Christmas cards. Inside she always writes a sweet note and adds a number. She's up to four birthdays since we saved her life."

"That must feel good when you get those."

"It does, but I wish I'd helped my partner more. Afterward, he wasn't the same. His physical wounds healed, but he never fully recovered emotionally and quit the force a year later. The post-traumatic stress took over his life, and he decided to go back to school to be a history teacher. Now he lives with his wife and three kids in the suburbs and rarely visits the city."

Skye smiled. "Sounds like he needed a quieter life. What about you? Do you miss city life?"

Bright headlights rounded the curve behind them. Jake glanced into the rearview mirror and held up a hand to shield his eyes from the glare, waiting for the high beams to drop to low, but instead, they continued to obscure his vision.

"Um...sometimes."

The truck sped toward them and as it drew closer the model resembled a Chevy 3500 series.

Jake accelerated, but the driver didn't slow.

"Hold on."

Three round lights flashed and raced toward their back bumper. Metal crunched and lurched them forward. Their seat belts caught and slammed them back into their seats. Shards of glass shattered to the floor.

Jake reached for his weapon out of habit but found his holster empty. His Glock was with Zain. Jake flipped the console lid open, retrieved his nine-millimeter and handed it to Skye.

"Can you shoot?"

She took the gun, checked the magazine, and then racked the slide, aiming out the broken back window. "Yeah, I can shoot."

When the truck came close again, she pulled the trigger in succession and took out all three lights on the front of the truck's grille. The driver backed off for a moment.

Skye popped the magazine again and counted

the rounds. "At least he can't blind us anymore, but he'll come back, and I only have about five bullets left."

Jake pressed the accelerator and tried to gain some distance while keeping his eye on the rearview mirror. "Where'd you learn to shoot?"

"Dad taught me. He used to take me to the gun range every Saturday. Said a girl can never be too careful. Did you not know I carried?"

"I do now. It looks like he's coming back."

"I can aim for his tires, but I doubt he'll stop."

The truck charged at them again. Skye raised the weapon and fired the rest of the bullets, taking out the windshield and one of his tires, but even her good aim did little to slow the assault.

The truck hit them harder than the first time. Jake lost control of the vehicle and ran off the road and down a steep embankment. Water splashed through the windows, dousing into the interior of the car. Crystal Creek swirled into the bottom of the SUV.

Skye grabbed his arm. "Jake. What do we do?"

"Scoot on top of the console and follow me out the driver side window."

She did as instructed, and he slipped his hand around her waist, pulling her with him. The water level rose inside but hadn't reached the side openings yet. Jake pressed his body onto the door frame, but gunfire sprayed across the floating car and forced him back into the sinking vehicle.

They moved to the passenger side of the SUV. Currents rocked and swayed the vehicle, carrying them toward the bridge. Water edged up to the bottom of the windows.

"When we get under the bridge, the current will flood the vehicle. Don't panic. Exit through the window and get out into the river as fast as you can, then swim for the pylon. We only have seconds before the car submerges."

Green water rolled white through the openings, filling the interior quicker than he expected. The shadow of the bridge shaded their escape. He nudged Skye toward the window. "Go now."

The power of the current pummeled the car, but he followed her, swimming through the force surging against him. The suction of the car pulled him farther down. He kicked, fighting the dark whirlpool determined to bury him in a watery grave.

He sank but kept his gaze upward. A strong hand gripped his wrist, pulling him toward the top. Skye's face emerged in distorted ripples.

Jake gulped in oxygen when he broke through the surface and Skye placed his hand on the rough concrete pylon. She placed a finger to her lips and pointed up toward the bridge. Men yelled commands, their shadows drifting from one side of the bridge to the other.

Skye leaned toward his ear and pointed. "They're waiting to see if we swim out from under the bridge. The car is still floating even though it's submerged. If we swim to the mound of storm debris piled over there in shallow water at the opposite end of the bridge, they won't see us, but we have to hurry."

"The ranch isn't far from here. If we make it to the debris, then we can sneak out through the thick brush on the bank and head back to Zain's. You ready?"

She nodded and sank into the water with a side dive. Skye didn't emerge until she reached the next pylon. Jake admired her strength and clarity under pressure. Most officers didn't have the fortitude she possessed.

Jake took a large breath, descended beneath the water, and followed her lead. One pylon down. Two to go.

Skye stayed hidden behind the hill of storm debris, hunkered down in the waters of Crystal Creek, and waited for Jake to emerge from the last section of the swim. Her injured leg ached from the exertion, but the external portion had healed and didn't pose any threat of infection.

Green bushes and overgrown brush covered the bank behind her. She tried not to think about what creatures might live there. Copperhead snakes loved to sunbathe on the rocky banks, but the Moore Family Ranch wasn't far.

The water broke and Jake shot up from underneath, gasping for air.

"That's the last one," she said.

"Thank goodness. I'm exhausted."

Skye pointed to the bank behind her. "We can stay hidden up until right before the grove of trees. We might be exposed for a split second."

"Let's hope they look the other way."

Skye followed Jake up the hill, and he stopped before the open area. She crouched down beside him. "We could wait until the sun goes down. We'd have a bit more cover."

He motioned toward the sunken vehicle, which had come to rest on a sandbar with the tail end pointing up. Two of the armed men stood on the opposite shoreline, their guns aimed at the water. "They're inspecting the car now. It won't be long until they realize our bodies aren't inside. When they do, they'll start looking for us. Once they dive down and find the car empty, they'll know we escaped and cover every area of this bridge. If we stay, we'll be sitting ducks."

Skye pointed toward the woods. "Then into the trees we go."

"We need to stay together." He took her hand in his. "On three. One, two, three."

Jake and Skye raced for the trees about one hundred yards away. They ran diagonally and uphill, over loose rock covering the dirt bank. Adrenaline rushed through Skye, alleviating the pain in her injured leg. Her breath dragged from overexertion. One of the men yelled, his voice echoing across the water. Gunshots fired, splintering bark off the trees. Jake clutched her hand tighter and pulled her faster up the hill.

"Hurry. They see us."

Skye lost her footing and slipped. A sharp rock cut into her knee, and a warm drip oozed down her leg. Jake pulled her hand, and she scrambled to regain her footing. Twenty feet until they were in the woods. More bullets pinged around them. Skye wanted to drop to the ground and cover her head, but Jake kept her moving. With one final stride, she lunged for the tree line and rolled into the safety of the secluded green canopy, landing on a grassy area. She paused to look at her knee.

"How bad is it?" Jake peered down at the cut.

"I'm fine."

He extended his hand and pulled her up. They ducked farther into the trees. "We've got to move. They'll be here soon, and I want to be far out of range."

Skye inhaled a quick breath of oxygen to calm her racing heart, which was pounding more from Jake's masculine protection than the short biathlon they'd completed. "Yeah. We definitely need to get some distance."

If only her heart would listen.

TWELVE

A couple of weeks later, Jake entered the modern gray building housing the Crystal Creek Sheriff's Department again. He was fully cleared to return to duty. Thanks to witnesses corroborating his account, the hearing wrapped up in record time. Internal Affairs had deemed his actions appropriate in regard to the imminent threat of his safety and the safety of nearby officers in the warehouse incident. He stepped off the elevator, continued down the hall and entered the main work area filled with desks, computers, large-monitor screens, and the smell of burned black coffee.

Nate handed him a cup when Jake reached his desk. "Well, how does it feel to be back?"

"Good." Jake lifted the cup. "Is this from Heather's?"

"Of course. I can't let you drink the toxic waste they fix here on your first day back. We've got to break you in slowly since you've been gone."

"It's only been a couple of weeks."

"You know all the officers at the warehouse gave statements to get the shooting board to release you quicker."

"I heard and I'm grateful, especially since I'm the new guy."

"Doesn't matter. You're one of us now."

The officers in Crystal Creek supported each other. The camaraderie mimicked a family, and Jake had never experienced a group like this one.

He took a sip of his coffee. "So, catch me up. Where are we at with the partial license plate tag off the motorcycles?"

"Looks like our buddy, Chad Wyndel—"

"You mean Kiam McClure?"

"Yeah, he's our guy. He owned a Honda CBR1000 Fireblade bike with a partial plate, HTN."

"The same one in Skye's drive-by shooting. Then he's the one running the ground attacks on Skye."

"Most likely. His prints weren't on the pizza box, but we traced the warehouse bar codes back to an IP address. Guess who it belongs to?"

"Kiam." Jake removed his blazer and hung it on the back of his chair before taking a seat.

"You would think so, but no." Nate said. "The data goes to a server owned by Mountain Shores Trust. The same company that owns Josephson Airfield. They print the bar code labels to look like the post office's. No one on the outside gets suspicious, then when whoever picks up the packages scans the bar code, the information goes to a private server of our dealer."

"Then whoever owns Mountain Shores Trust is the money man pulling all the strings and giving Kiam his instructions. Maybe we can get Kiam to tell us who signs his paycheck. My guess is Dante Carello."

"And that's why I brought you coffee today. I got the arrest warrant. Wanna go pick Kiam up?"

"You got an address?" Jake took another sip of his espresso-laden jolt.

"Of course."

"Then what are we waiting for? Let's go get this guy."

Nate hesitated. "We might want to take some backup. This kid doesn't live in the best of neighborhoods."

"Which one are we talking?"

"Magnolia View."

Jake scanned the room and motioned to another detective team. "Hardy and Lowe, care to give us a hand with an arrest at MV?"

The two seasoned detectives nodded and joined them. Glen Hardy and Reina Lowe were an interesting pair who had been working together for years. They had solved a myriad of murders in the area, and respect proceeded them in most neighborhoods.

After driving for fifteen minutes, Jake steered their car to building F and peered up five stories. "Of course, he lives on the top level."

"Better up there than down here."

Jake followed Nate's gaze to the ground floor. Large men huddled in groups at the corners of the buildings, and some wandered out from the shadows when the detectives stepped from their cars. He made sure his badge hung around his neck in plain view and placed his hand on the grip of his gun.

The men took a step back when Jake moved toward the stairs. "Which unit on the top floor?"

"Five seventeen."

The other two cops moved behind them, keeping an eye on their backs. They climbed to the fifth floor, down a corridor open on both ends, and found Kiam's apartment. Jake retrieved his weapon, raised a fist, and pounded on the door. "Crystal Creek Sheriff. Open up."

Seconds passed with no answer. Jake tried again. "Kiam McClure? Open up. We have a few questions."

Still nothing. Jake tried the knob. The door opened, and he entered the dark apartment, followed by the others.

The strong stench of death greeted them and lingered as they cleared each room. Jake moved farther down a hallway and pressed open the door to a back bedroom.

Kiam's body was facedown, the carpet underneath him stained red. "He's in here."

The other three officers moved into the room. Nate stepped past Jake for a closer look. "That's not good. We thought he was our guy."

"He may still be. Just because someone killed him doesn't mean he hasn't been the one tormenting Skye."

Hardy picked up a key off the dresser. "Looks like a storage unit key. I saw some when we first arrived. Reina and I will go check it out."

Jake nodded as they left, then he pulled on gloves and opened the nightstand drawer next to the bed. "He's got a gun. Nine-millimeter. Did the ballistics ever come back on the slugs we submitted from the drive-by shooting?"

"Let me check." Nate pulled out his phone and tapped the screen. "Yep, nine-millimeter."

"So, Kiam shot at us."

"We can turn in the gun, make sure the slugs you collected match this weapon. You know, someone else is pulling the strings behind all this or the kid wouldn't be dead. If only we'd gotten to him first. He could've shared information on the Carello cartel, but with him lifeless on the carpet, we've missed our chance."

"Maybe not." Jake pulled a photo from the desk drawer. "Why would Kiam McClure have a photo of Lorna Daly at the top of Crystal Creek Falls?"

Nate placed the gun in an evidence bag. "Is she the girl who fell and died when we were in high school?"

"Yeah." Jake flipped over the image. "And this picture was taken the day she died. Don't you find it odd that our kid, who was probably in middle school at the time the photo was taken, keeps this in the top drawer of his nightstand?"

"There's got to be a connection."

"Yeah. But what? Somebody didn't want him talking." Jake squatted next to the body and pointed to the man's arm. "He's got the same skull tattoo associated with the Carellos, and I caught a brief glimpse of the truck driver who ran us off the road. This is our guy."

"You think Dante Carello pushed the girl from the top and Kiam found out, so they killed him?"

"That's one theory." Jake pointed to bruising on the man's knuckles and jaw. "Looks like he put up a fight. But we still don't know if he was the one who stabbed Randy."

"I'll call Natalie and have her come investigate the body. Maybe she'll find something to help. Whoever decided to keep Kiam quiet is the same person trying to silence Skye. If we can find some DNA evidence here, then we may be able to stop our money man before he kills again."

Hardy reentered the bedroom. "Y'all might want to come take a look at this."

Jake and Nate followed the seasoned detective back outside, down to the ground floor and out to a bank of storage units located in the middle of the parking lot. Hardy stopped by the one marked 517, slipped in the storage key and turned the lock. "I never expected to find this."

With a quick pull on the door, the storage building opened and Hardy flipped a light switch.

"Well. What do ya know? Kiam drives our truck." Jake walked around the outside of the vehicle. The grille lights had been removed, but the bullet holes still lived in the metal hood. "Good work, man."

"That's not all."

Hardy pulled a tarp off another object parked to the side. "We found the Honda CBR1000 Fireblade bike."

"And all our loose ends tie up with the dead guy. The truck that ran us off the road, the motorcycle driver who shot at us and even the gun they used. Everything ends here with Kiam," Jake said.

Nate walked around the truck. "Whoever's behind this set the kid up good."

"Yeah, too good. We're back at square one, except for the photo of Lorna and Mountain Shores Trust, which we haven't been able to trace." Jake headed back upstairs, determined to find something more in Kiam's apartment. He couldn't let their case freeze up here.

* * *

Skye leaned against the inside of the corral fence and cheered when Romi rode by on the miniature pony Bryn Cavanaugh had trailered over for her daughter's riding lesson.

"Thank you so much for doing this, Bryn. She's been missing Coco so much."

"Coco has missed her, and I'm happy to help any way I can, especially with all the tragedy you've been through lately. I'm still shocked about Penny getting arrested."

"She's innocent. They released her not long after she got there, but when she walked into the building, my heart sank. I'm glad she wasn't involved. We've been friends for years, and I don't know what I'd do without her, even if things are a little strained between us at the moment."

"I'm sure she'll come around. You, Carli and Penny were inseparable in college."

Skye nudge Bryn with her elbow. "And you spent all your time with Walter. I don't think I've ever seen two people more in love."

A smile curled her friend's lips. "Yes, and we still are."

"What's the hubs up to today while you're out here giving private lessons?"

"He's flying to Kentucky to purchase a couple of new horses. We needed a few more to keep growing our breeding business."

"Wow. Business must be good."

Bryn brushed a strand of hair from her face. "I can hardly keep up."

"Speaking of flying, have you ever heard of Josephson Airfield? I think it's a private strip near the edge of town."

Bryn shook her head. "No. Why?"

"Someone mentioned it the other day, and in all my years growing up here, I still didn't know about the place."

"There's probably lots of places around here we've never heard of." Bryn stepped toward the middle of the ring to give Romi a few instructions.

People all over the state sought out her friend's training. The woman had grown up in her family's horse business. After her father passed away last June, Bryn had taken the fledgling business to a new level in a matter of months. Romi was blessed to be trained by such an experienced rider.

"Good job, Romi. Let's move Coco into a trot and do two more circles, then we can finish up."

After the lesson and Bryn headed home, Skye returned with Romi to the guesthouse for some lunch. She pulled lettuce, tomato, ham, and cheese from the fridge and placed the ingredients on the counter when a knock rapped against the door.

Penny stood outside, holding a basket of fresh fruit and chicken salad sandwiches. "I had to come by, plead my case, and bribe you with lunch. I can't bear the thought of not talking."

Skye pulled her longtime friend into a hug. "Me either, and I'm so glad you're okay. I owe you an apology for not standing up for you at the warehouse. I was in shock."

"That makes two of us." They moved into the kitchen, and Penny placed the basket of goodies on the counter. "I never expected to get arrested for doing my job. What was Jake thinking?"

Skye returned her sandwich ingredients to the fridge and grabbed a few glasses from the cabinet. "He didn't have a choice."

"But I've known him for years. We grew up together. Remember all the camping trips into the mountains and sitting around the fire with everyone? He knows me, and for him to arrest me like that... I didn't know what to do."

The trauma of the entire situation weighed on Skye. "You know I believe you, but in his defense, you did walk into a warehouse holding mass quantities of fentanyl. He really didn't have a choice but to arrest you until he gathered more information."

Skye pulled out one of the bar stools, added a few grapes to her plate and sipped her tea.

"I know, but I was so embarrassed." Penny took a seat beside her. "Why do you think Cale sent me there? Do you think he knew?"

Their postmaster oversaw multiple post office branches in the area. Skye liked him even if he had ambitions and would climb over others to increase his position. At least he kept expectations consistent and treated all his employees with respect. "Cale's the ultimate professional. Had he known the contents of those shipments, then agents from the Office of the Inspector General would've busted down the doors with the feds a long time ago."

Penny took a bite of her sandwich. "I've never seen so many drugs in one place like that before, and they were running the operation as a legitimate business."

"Tell me more about Kiam. What's he like?"

Penny swallowed. "Who?"

"Sorry, I meant Chad."

"He's quiet and doesn't say much but tatted up and strong. He's able to lift large packages with no problem and does his work. He shows up on time and gets the job done. Cale loves him. Do you think he's involved in this or got involved in something accidentally?"

"I think he's involved. Jake and his team are trying to locate his whereabouts. Chad faked the address in his work records, and he used a fake name."

"Chad Wyndel isn't his real name?"

"Try Kiam McClure."

Penny raised her eyebrows. "Maybe they'll find him soon and this will all be over."

Skye glanced back at Romi, who was playing on the floor. She knew better than to get her hopes up. Even if Kiam was involved, he was a middleman, a low-level transporter. The threat on their lives extended high above him, and they still had no idea who had targeted them for death.

THIRTEEN

Jake knocked on Skye's door and tried to think of the best way to tell her about Kiam. Every one of their possible leads had imploded with the kid's death, and they were no closer to discovering the mastermind behind the threats on her life. But there was more he wanted to tell her.

After taking a swim in the river, he was done letting the fear of his father's sins shape who he was. He loved Skye and wanted to place everything on the table. He wasn't sure if he would make a good father, but for the first time in his life he was willing to try.

He knocked on the door again, trying not to spill the two coffees he held in his left hand. Maybe Zain was right. The break from the case was good and had provided him with some perspective on the details regarding Skye.

The front door swung open. Sully rushed out and circled Jake, sniffing him. He reached down with his free hand and scratched between the dog's ears. "Hey, buddy. I'm the good guy. You don't have to sniff me."

"That's debatable," a female voice said.

Jake glanced up. Penny stood with her arms folded across her chest.

"Oh. Hey. What are you doing here?"

"Well, after my little trip to the police station a couple of weeks ago, where they confiscated all my belongings, fingerprinted me and tossed me into a smelly interrogation room for hours, no thanks to you, Nate let me go. The postmaster corroborated my story, vouched for my willingness to be a team player, and told them I was only doing my job by filling in for Chad—or Kiam, whatever his name is. I had some paperwork and errands today and decided to visit one of my dearest friends to make sure she didn't believe the lies that have been circulating about me. We just finished up lunch."

Jake shifted his weight during the long diatribe. "You know, I was only doing my job. Arresting you wasn't personal."

"Sure felt personal."

She didn't budge from the center of the doorway, nor did she invite him inside. Penny wasn't going to make this moment easy. Maybe he should go. This was not the time to bare his soul to Skye, especially when one of her best friends held a grudge and probably had filled her head with negative words about him.

He tried again. "I had to do my job. You were caught at a warehouse, picking up a shipment of fentanyl to be distributed. Had any other driver walked through the door, I would've arrested them, too."

"But you know me. We went to school together, and when I told you I was filling in for Chad, I expected you to believe me."

"The law doesn't care about my school history. And as for Kiam, he was involved. We found him dead in his apartment this morning."

Penny straightened at the news, her hand flying to cover her open mouth. "What? That's awful."

Skye stepped around the corner. "What's awful?"

Jake's gaze shifted to her and his palms began to sweat. Maybe it was from the coffee he held.

"Here. I brought this from Heather's. Penny, if I'd known you were here, I would've grabbed one for you too."

"Sure you would have."

Skye took the cup. "Thanks. Now tell us about Kiam."

Jake leaned back against the post, picturing this whole situation differently in his head, but he might as well fill her in on the details. "We went to arrest Kiam this morning and found his body in the apartment. We also found the truck used to force us off the road, the motorcycle our culprit drove in his utility shed, and the gun that shot you in his nightstand."

Skye stepped onto the porch and leaned against the outer wall of the house across from him. "He's the one who's been trying to kill me."

"All wrapped up in a neat little bow." Jake sipped his coffee.

"Well, that's not what I hoped to hear."

"At least you won't have to be afraid anymore and can move back to your house," Penny said.

Jake held up his hand. "Actually, we still think Skye's in danger."

"Because whoever killed Kiam did so to keep him quiet and that person is the one funding all the attempts on my life, correct?"

"Pretty much."

"And with all the leads tied up, we aren't any closer to finding out who killed Randy. In fact, you came to tell me we're back at the beginning."

Jake nodded. "There are a few other things I'd like to discuss with you—in private, when you have time."

Penny glanced at her watch, then stepped back inside the open door to grab her purse and keys. "I can take a hint. Besides, I've got to get back to work. I'll call ya later."

"Thanks for lunch." Skye gave her friend a hug.

When Penny walked past Jake, she leaned in close. "You're still not off the hook," she said, then bounced down the steps, hopped in her car and left.

Skye motioned to a couple of rockers and sipped her coffee. "Don't mind her. She's still reeling over the warehouse arrest, but she'll get over it. One thing I love about Penny is that she's quick to forgive."

"Good to know. What about you? Are you quick to forgive?"

"Depends on the situation. Have you done something else you need forgiveness for?"

"Nothing at the moment but give me a little time and I'll probably do something." He pointed to her knee. "How's the gash?"

"Better than last week. It hurts every time I walk but seems to be healing now. We have much to be thankful for."

This was the perfect opportunity to bring up the subject. "We do, and I've been thinking a lot about us during my time off." Jake reached for her hand, but she leaned forward, wrapping her fingers around the paper cup.

"I've been thinking, too. About leaving."

He struggled with her announcement. They always seemed to be going in opposite directions. He came near, she pulled away and vice versa. He tried not to react and listened instead.

"I could take Romi somewhere Carello can't find us. I wasn't sure we were going to escape the river alive, and the thought of never seeing my daughter again is too much to bear. I need to take her somewhere safe, far away from Crystal Creek."

Tension filled his chest with her suggestion. "I know we're back at square one, but we can stop them if we stick together."

"Even if I identify the killer as a member of the Carello cartel and you put him away, they'll still keep coming after us. You know there are a hundred Kiam McClures out there. The danger doesn't end and living in their backyard doesn't help. If we enter witness protection, at least we'll have a chance. Do you think you could arrange a meeting with a US Marshal?"

He stood, walked to the railing on the porch and gripped the top bar with his hands. He couldn't bear for her to leave. Not like this. Not before he told her his true feelings.

"Witness protection's a serious decision. You have to cut ties with everyone and everything you love, and Romi will have to live under another name. We would never be able to see each other again. Are you willing to do that?"

"If it keeps her safe, I'll do anything."

The US Marshals' office worked with departments across the country to keep American citizens safe from drug cartels and murderers who wanted to keep witnesses quiet, but if Skye chose to enter the program, any relationship he had with her would end.

Jake wasn't ready to let her go. "If we can dismantle the cartel, maybe disappearing to another part of the country won't be necessary."

"Do you think their organization can be completely destroyed?"

"We've been able to bring down other cartels, and with the Charlotte office willing to partner with us, our resources have doubled." He moved back to the rocker and perched on the edge, hoping she'd change her mind. "We'll get these guys, but you can't leave—not yet."

"I'm not sure Romi and I have another option."

"Actually, there's more options than you think." He held out his hand. "Take a ride with me."

She glanced past him toward the driveway where he parked the ATV. "In a side-by-side?"

"I asked Zain if we could borrow one of the ranch's vehicles and he gave me this one. I thought we might have some fun after everything that's happened. With the internal investigation over, I want to celebrate and thought you might join me. Plus, Zain wants us to check the perimeter of the ranch while we're out. Romi can come, too, if you want. We won't leave the confines of the property."

"She's over playing at Eli's." Her gaze cut back to the ATV. "Only if I can drive."

If relinquishing the keys is what it took for

her to go with him then he would give up driving. "Deal."

He held up the keys and snatched them back when she reached for them. "You do know how to drive one of these things, right?"

"Of course. I'm a great driver."

She reached for the keys again, but he didn't open his fist. "Better than me?"

She grabbed his wrist, lowered his hand, and pried open his fingers. "Always."

With a flash of a smile, Skye left him standing on the porch and hopped in the vehicle. "Coming?"

He'd let her drive anywhere if doing so kept them together.

Skye revved the engine and drove faster across the pastureland of the Moore Family Ranch. Wind whipped around them, and she grinned at Jake's white knuckles gripping the side bar.

"You're not scared are you, Detective?"

"Me? Nah. But you might want to slow down for that dip up—"

Too late. The divot in the landscape sent them airborne, and they landed with a thud. She steered the wheels hard right when they hit the ground and spun them into a doughnut. "This thing is fun. Romi would love it. Maybe I'll see if we can give rides to the kids for her birthday party tomorrow. You're coming right?"

"Didn't know I was invited."

"Of course, you are. Romi adores you."

"I should be able to come." Jake grabbed the side bar again when she hit the gas out of her circle and raced toward the covered bridge. "Seems like you've driven one of these before."

"My father always had four-wheelers on the farmland. Penny, Carli, and I used to go mudding in them after a good summer thunderstorm. We'd be covered head to toe in dirt when we got back home. Used to make my momma so mad. She'd take a garden hose to me before she'd let me come inside and mess up her house with my disgusting clothes. Talk about some good memories."

"How come you never invited me and Randy to go mudding with y'all? We had our own ATVs."

"Some things you just have to do with your girlfriends. No boys allowed."

He motioned ahead. "Let's go through the covered bridge."

Skye steered toward the structure and crossed onto the wooden slats. Shade engulfed them and relieved the hot afternoon sun while the white rapids of the creek rushed underneath, cooling the temperature a few degrees more. She drove to the end and turned off the engine. For a moment, they remained in silence, taking in the spread of pastureland, blue sky and the backdrop of majestic mountains. A lone hawk swooped down into the field and back up again. Jake climbed from the vehicle and moved around to her side.

"Zain's property line is about another fifty yards down the creek bank then through those trees over to the main road. Wanna walk with me?"

He held out his hand, and she slipped her fingers into his palm, expecting him to let go once she stood, but he kept her hand in his. They walked in silence along the curve of the creek bank, absorbing the babble of water spilling over stones smoothed by constant agitation, mimicking the trials and troubles of life. God often used friction to smooth flaws in her heart, shaping the mistakes into something beautiful.

Jake squeezed her hand. "Most of the decisions I've made in my life have been influenced by my father's actions during my childhood."

He exhaled and kept his eyes on the path. Not wanting to rush the moment, she waited for him to continue. He never talked much about his dad, and she hoped her silence encouraged him to share.

"Most of the time, I've painted my dad in a negative light, but the truth is, he wasn't always mean to me. I have some early memories of times he took me fishing in this creek or tossed a baseball in the backyard."

"I'm glad you had some good times with him."

"Me, too, even though things deteriorated after he got fired from the police force. He changed and started drinking, then cheated on my mom. When she confronted him about his behavior, he'd fly into a rage and hit her. As I got older and larger, I stepped in between them more often than not and took the beatings for her. She tried to get him to stop, but he was too strong for both of us."

Skye motioned to the ground where a small brook flowed into Crystal Creek. Jake stepped across first then helped her make the small leap. His strong arms caught her and held her for a moment before he continued along the path, keeping her hand in his.

"At first, I never hit him back. But one night, he wouldn't leave my mom alone. Nothing I said or did distracted him from his attack and... I punched him."

His gaze remained straight ahead, his jaw tight and eyes narrowed, as if he were back in the room with his father.

"I'll never forget the look in his eyes when he realized I'd hit him. I'm not sure if he or I was more shocked and hurt. I always promised myself I'd never lose control, never hit him, but I did."

Jake shook his head, pausing for a moment. "Then my father came at me with a fierce rage. For the first time, I defended myself and my mom. Randy was with me when it all started. I guess he left at some point and ran to get his father. When they came back…"

Jake's voice choked up, and he stopped walking, fighting for composure.

Skye grieved for him. No child should ever have to deal with so much trauma in their life. Even now, as an adult, the memories still haunted Jake. What kind of man would treat his child with such violence?

Skye stepped in front of him, taking his other hand in hers. "We don't have to talk about this. I don't need the details."

"You need to know the truth, what kind of man I am." His gaze locked on hers, fighting back tears. "It was me. I was the one Randy had to stop, not my father. They had to pull me off him. He almost died because once I started hitting him, I didn't stop."

An icy wave rolled through her. She stepped back and dropped his hands.

"I understand if you don't want me around anymore," he said.

She wasn't sure what to say. Randy had never told her the details. He'd let her assume the usual—Jake's father attacked his son again, and they stepped in to stop the fight. "It's not that. I never knew. Randy didn't say anything to me about—"

"I asked him not to tell anyone. Instead, they

took my father to the hospital. He was in intensive care for three days. Randy's dad got my mom into a women's shelter, where she received counseling, financial assistance, and an educational grant to learn a new trade and provide for both of us. While she completed her nursing degree, I lived with Randy's family. When Dad got out of the hospital, he left town. I haven't heard from or seen him since."

"I remember being worried about you. I came to Randy's house, but he said you were sleeping."

Jake bent down and took a smooth stone between his fingers, flinging the rock across the water's surface. "I didn't want to see anyone. My father landed a few good shots, too. He blackened my eyes and busted my lip, but physical wounds heal much easier than emotional ones."

A moment passed.

Jake straightened next to her. "Randy wanted me to tell you. He said you had a right to know the truth. I realized how much he loved you and knew he could give you the kind of life you deserved. The life I couldn't provide, so I left."

Skye paced a few steps away, letting the truth of the situation hit her for the first time. Jake had given her up. "You left because Randy loved me?"

She took a seat on a boulder, the enormity of his choice grieving her heart again. She was right back in the past, when he'd left her standing alone in his driveway.

"I wanted a good life for you. I couldn't give you that."

"But I loved you. And you made a life-altering decision without even including me in the conversation. You and Randy decided my future."

"I wasn't ready to get married back then. You wanted a family. You dreamed of having children and wanted a husband. I couldn't give you that, but Randy could."

She stood, turned her back and swiped away the tears from under her eyes. A gentle breeze stirred the leaves in the trees and dried the wetness on her cheeks. "I don't know what to say. In one respect, I'm furious you gave up on us, and in another I'm impressed with the selfless love you showed Randy."

Jake pulled her into his chest, his arms wrapping around her. She breathed in the faded scent of his woodsy cologne, luring her to love him again, far deeper than she'd ever imagined. His arms belonged around her, but there was one thing she wanted more than Jake…a safe life for her daughter.

She stepped back, breaking the moment. "Why are you telling me this now? Have you changed your mind about having a family?"

His eyes searched hers for a moment. "I know I want to be with you."

"Like before? When you left? I've got Romi, and I can't go back to where we left off."

He pushed his hands into his pockets and shook his head. "Do we have to define all the details tonight? Why can't we agree to spend time together, the three of us, and see what happens?"

Skye scanned the horizon, all the pain and memories of their past flooding back. "Romi deserves better and so do I."

"I made a vow to never be like my father and I'm getting there, but I need a little more time."

"It's been seven years, Jake. How much time do you need?" Skye swiped her cheeks again. "If you didn't want a future with me then, how can I trust you now?"

"I don't know. I can only tell you I'm willing to try."

Skye turned back toward the bridge. "I can't do this again. I won't do this again."

He touched her arm and turned her to face him, his eyes searching hers. "Then where does that leave us?"

She didn't want to say for fear they'd never be able to move past the line drawn in the sand, but what choice did she have? "Friends?"

He rolled his eyes and turned away from her. "Like that always works out well."

She tried again. "Without a commitment, there is no us, Jake. Surely you can understand that my heart can't take any more loss."

His demeanor softened and he reached out to tuck a strand of hair from her face. "I do."

He pulled her into his arms and kissed the top of her head. Decisions like these were never easy and she almost wavered as he held her there, but she had to protect her heart this time. She had to protect Romi.

Jake released her and walked back toward the ATV then climbed into the driver's seat, his body slumped. "We need to finish checking the perimeter and then I'll take you back home."

Her line in the sand expanded into a full-fledged wall.

Skye climbed into the vehicle and held on tightly as Jake scoured the boundaries for any signs of a breach. They sped past horses grazing in nearby fields and barns dotting the landscape, letting silence fill the gulf between them.

She struggled to focus on anything other than Jake's words replaying in her head. Had she made the right decision for her and Romi?

Jake pointed toward an area where the tall grass flattened in two parallel lines. "Looks like someone's pulled off here."

He stopped the vehicle and climbed out. Large tire tracks in the mud ran along the edge of the property and then back onto the main road.

"They parked here for a while, then spun their tires when they drove back up to the asphalt."

Jake took out his phone and snapped a few photos. "These tires are large, like Kiam's."

"Then he followed us back here?"

"If he did, let's hope he didn't share that with the man who killed him."

"I don't know where else we'd go. I'm out of places to stay unless we hide out in a hotel, and without working, I can't afford the expense. My saving's account is dwindling faster than I hoped."

"You can stay with me. I've got a farm similar to Zain's, just a bit smaller. We have top-notch security. There's a small apartment over the garage, and the contractors finished the remodel a couple of days ago. Mom moved into her new mother-in-law suite, so the space is available."

"I'm not sure that's a good idea."

"Nonsense." His tone carried a bit of punch. "That's what friends are for."

She ignored his remark. Friends or not, she hoped she and Romi could remain at the Moore Family Ranch. The last thing she wanted to do was move again, disrupting Romi's life even more.

FOURTEEN

Night air swirled through the open windows of the safehouse's enclosed sunroom, and Jake rubbed his burning eyes. He zoomed in on the tire treads again on his laptop. The imprints didn't match the model of Kiam's truck from the bridge, a Chevy Silverado 3500 series. They were larger, which might work in their favor. If he matched the custom tires to the same truck models sold in the area, then his search results would narrow the pool of suspects.

He rubbed his face, closed the lid, and decided to wait until morning, when his mind wasn't so exhausted.

Light from the laptop snapped off, darkening the room. His body relaxed. Romi's birthday party was tomorrow, and he still had to put the finishing touches on her present. He planned to take the morning off, but now he also wanted to run the search. Maybe Nate could check the photos and he could focus on completing Ro-mi's gift.

A thump landed against the wall. Jake shot up and glanced at his phone. Two in the morning. His senses heightened, and he peered through the window into the main living area. Sully trotted over to his bowl and lapped his water.

He exhaled and rested his head back against the pillow then closed his eyes again. He had to get some sleep if the dog could stay quiet.

Sully let out a low growl, transforming into a bark when an interior floorboard creaked. Jake grabbed his weapon and cuffs, slid from the couch, and moved to the doorway leading into the main living area. A shadowed figure crept down the hall from the back utility room and crossed toward the steps.

Jake slipped inside the door, flattening against the walls to camouflage himself in the darkness. Sully growled again, then moved to his bowl, chewing something tasty the intruder tossed in-side.

With his gun raised, Jake took a step and pushed the barrel against the man's upper back. The suspect never saw him and halted his move-ments.

"Put your hands in the air…slowly."

The man lifted his arms, revealing a skull tat-too. Jake reached for his wrist to slap on the cuffs, but with a swift turn, the man grabbed the slide of the gun and wrestled for control.

The weapon fell and slid across the floor. With a strong lunge, the intruder slammed into Jake, cracked his back against the kitchen counter and landed a punch to his jaw. Jake fought back with a flurry of punches to his attacker's torso, but the intruder kept him pinned. The man didn't flinch from multiple hits to his side.

A red-hot frenzy surged through Jake. He landed a strong knee to his attacker's gut and shoved him back. They fell across an end table, sending a lamp to the ground. Glass broke and littered the floor, but he continued to fight.

He wrestled the man to the ground, his father's face flashing through his mind with each blow stronger than the next. His focus cleared with each hit. The man covered his head, fending off the assault, but Jake didn't stop. Instead, he straddled him, knocking him unconscious and pulled back his fist again, ready to finish him off with one last hit.

Stop.

The word vibrated strong through him. His fist paused in midair. The intruder didn't move, blacked out from his previous blows. He pulled his cuffs from his pants and placed them on the man's wrists.

"Jake?" Skye's voice broke through his haze of anger, her eyes wide at the sight of the intruder. She rushed down the steps and knelt by the injured man's side, pressing two fingers to his neck. "Is he dead?"

Jake fell back against the wall, trying to catch his breath. He rubbed his knuckles, bloodied from his self-imposed punishment. "He came to kill you."

"He has a pulse." She shot him a worried look, then grabbed her phone and dialed 911 on speaker. "My name is Skye Anderson. We are at 524 Moore Ranch Road. Please hurry. There's been an intruder, and he's injured."

"Are you harmed, ma'am?" the operator asked.

"No, but the intruder is unconscious. He's been beaten."

"By you?"

Skye glanced at Jake and he nodded. "By the detective who's at my house."

"What's the detective's name?"

Jake leaned toward the phone. "Detective Reed, badge number 451. The intruder tried to take my gun and we fought."

"Patrol is on the way."

Skye placed the phone on the stairs, opened the refrigerator and retrieved several bags of frozen vegetables. She placed one on the man's jaw and another on his eye. Jake watched for any signs of conscious aggression. If the man stirred or moved so much as a pinkie toward her, he'd be back on him, but his enemy remained motionless except for the rise and fall of his chest.

Skye lifted the man's cuffed arms and touched the tattoo with her fingers. "Do you think he's the one who killed Randy?"

"Maybe. But a lot of the Carello members have the same tattoo. Any one of them could be Randy's murderer. The only way to know for sure—"

"Is if I remember his face. I know." She studied the man. "He doesn't look familiar, and he seems young. For some reason, I feel like the man from our accident is older and bigger, too."

"Why do you think that?"

"Nothing much, but something about the skin on his hands. He had more wrinkles and prominent veins. Not smooth like this young guy. And he wore a ring."

"A ring? You've never mentioned any jewelry before."

"It was black and gold. I don't remember the design on it."

She took a seat beside him and lifted his hand in hers, placing a frozen bag of peas across his right hand.

"Thanks," he said.

"Are you okay?"

Jake glanced at the man again and thought of the night with his father. "I will be."

"You stopped him from getting to Romi, and for that I'm thankful, but his injuries are severe."

"And if I hadn't stopped him, your injuries would be fatal." A rush of heat climbed through him. Maybe he had gone a little too far, but the man still had a pulse. Wasn't that enough?

"When did you come down the stairs?"

"I woke up and heard a commotion. When I got to the landing, you had your fist in the air, but you didn't hit him. You put handcuffs on him instead, and then I came down after he was restrained."

"And Romi?"

Skye's gaze glassed over. He wanted to comfort her, but she had been clear about their relationship—or friendship. Whatever she wanted to call the distance between them.

"She's still asleep for now. I'm guessing sirens and blue lights might wake her up. I don't want her to see any of this. She still has nightmares from the accident and doesn't need any more trauma."

His body relaxed with relief, knowing Romi hadn't witnessed any of the violence. "Let's hope she sleeps through the sirens, too."

They sat in silence for a moment, Jake still reliving the scene in his mind. The man had taken his gun right from his hands. Only trained assassins, cops, or military wielded defensive tactics like that. In past encounters with Carello's members, they lacked fighting skills. They used all kinds of weapons—even traded in them—but this man had showed precision and an effective sparring technique, despite the skull tattoo on his arm.

Loud footsteps slammed on the outside porch. Zain stepped through the front door and scanned the room. "Are y'all okay?"

"We're fine," Skye said, "but this man's going to need to be taken to the hospital."

Her concern for the man shot straight through Jake. After the night with his father, he'd vowed to never let his rage take over again or let anyone see him lose control. Tonight, he'd exposed Skye to both, and from Zain's expression, he hoped his actions didn't trigger another Internal Affairs investigation.

Zain moved to the man's side and checked his respirations and pulse. "He should be okay. The ambulance is on the way."

A movement at the top of the stairwell shifted everyone's focus.

"Mommy?"

Skye turned at the sound of her daughter's voice, rushed to Romi and lifted the little girl into her arms, then disappeared around the corner.

Zain stepped over the body and moved next to Jake, leaning in close. "Your first night back on guard duty and an assassin breaks in. What are the chances of that?"

"Zero to none, but this guy was headed upstairs, where Romi and Skye slept. If we hadn't been here, the guy would've killed them both."

His friend rubbed the back of his neck, probably walking through all the scenarios they would encounter when the sheriff got wind of Jake's actions. Jake hoped Internal Affairs didn't decide to pull the entire department for an inquiry—or worse, question Zain's leadership. The man outperformed every previous supervisor Jake had worked under.

"At least you didn't have a weapon on you. Maybe we can get him to talk since you didn't kill him."

Jake pointed toward his secondary gun lying on the floor across the room. "He knocked my piece from my hand, or he would be dead. I did what was needed to keep Skye and Romi safe. I doubt he'll talk, anyway. His skill level matched mine. Might've been even better had he been a bit stronger. The man swiped the gun right out of my hands."

"Are you saying he was a professional?"

"He was trained by someone good. His moves were quick and accurate, and he put up a fight."

"And you didn't shoot him?"

"I didn't have a chance, not once he turned on me. Is someone new training Carello's members?"

"Not that I know of. Last I heard, Dante hired thugs, but their fighting skills never matched ours. From the looks of this man's face, neither did he."

"My tactical training kicked in."

Zain shot Jake a sarcastic look.

"What? I had to stop him from harming Skye."

"You did more than stop him. You pummeled him. Don't get me wrong, I'm thankful they're safe, but your decisions lately have pushed the boundaries of protocol. It's one thing when you shoot a man who's charging a fork truck at you, but what's the sheriff going to say when he finds out you beat a man half to death?"

"I saved two lives tonight, and the guy attacked me. He resisted arrest, and he didn't die. You and I both know Carello is going to keep sending assassins. This location's blown and the focus shouldn't be on me. Where are we going to send Skye and Romi?"

"Let me figure that out. You head home tonight and come by the office in the morning. We'll make sure all this gets briefed correctly."

Jake stood, tossed the now-thawed bag of peas into the sink, and stretched his hand. "Send them with me. My farm has almost as much security as the ranch. Throw in a few guards, and I can keep them safe until we wrap up the investigation."

"They'll be fine tonight. This place will be crawling with officers in about two minutes. I want to process the scene, gather all the evidence and then I'll make a decision about where to move them."

Sirens grew louder and announced the arrival of reinforcements. Jake looked at the stairs and decided to save any arguments for the morning.

He made his way up to the second level and stopped in the hallway outside Romi's room. He peered inside, where pink dominated the color scheme. Skye sat on the edge of her daughter's bed. Jake remained quiet, not wanting to interrupt the sweet moment.

"What happened downstairs, Mommy?"

"Everything's okay, my sweet. Close your eyes and go back to sleep."

"Is Mr. Jakey okay? I saw him sitting on the floor. He looked sad."

Skye pulled the covers up over her daughter's little body and tucked the spread around her. "He's fine."

"What about the other man lying on the floor? He didn't look so good."

"That man made a bad mistake and will be heading to jail. Mr. Jake protected us."

Romi grabbed her stuffed horse and hugged the toy to her chest. "Just like Daddy used to do."

Jake watched Skye brush a strand of hair from her daughter's face. "Yes. Just like Daddy used to do. Now go back to sleep. I love you."

The little girl's words pierced his soul. He

might've protected them, but he was nothing like Randy.

Jake retreated into the hall, his heart heavy. Romi had seen what he'd done to the man downstairs. She'd seen the violence Jake caused. The first time he saw his father hit someone, the event had traumatized him. And now he'd done the same to Romi.

He needed to leave, figure out his next move. If only he'd stayed in Charlotte instead of returning and reopening Randy's case, then Skye wouldn't be in this situation. Maybe Zain was right. His lack of self-control not only injured an intruder, but his temper and choices had endangered the two most important people in his life. He was more like his father than he'd ever planned to be.

After Romi fell back to sleep, Skye returned to the main living area. The paramedic rolled the intruder's stretcher toward the door. Bags of fluid dangled from an intravenous pole near the man's head, while an oxygen mask covered his face but did little to hide his bruising and swollen tissues.

She scanned the space, looking for Jake, but didn't see him. A few officers still milled about, including Zain, but Jake was gone. He hadn't even said goodbye.

Zain finished up a conversation and stepped

over to where she stood. "I think we're about to wrap up here. How's Romi?"

"She finally fell back to sleep, but she asked a lot of questions about everything here." Skye pointed at the mess. "Can I get this glass cleaned up before someone steps on a piece and gets injured?"

"Go ahead. We've collected everything we need from the scene."

"Do you know where Jake went?"

"I told him to head home so he can meet me first thing in the morning, but he said he wanted to tell you goodbye. Last time I saw him, he was headed upstairs."

"He must've changed his mind, because I never saw him." Glass crunched under her flip-flops. "Tell Carli I'm so sorry about all this. Her guesthouse is in shambles."

"Don't worry about her. We're thankful nothing happened to you and Romi tonight. I'm not sure how the intruder got past both guards, but we'll figure everything out in the morning. In the meantime, you'll have two extra guards outside for the rest of the night."

"Thanks." Skye entered the kitchen and reached for the broom, then swept up the pieces of the broken lamp, still thinking about Jake. With all their leads ending with Kiam and Jake in the friend zone, her desire to leave Crystal Creek with Romi was stronger than ever.

Zain squatted down and gripped the handle of the dustpan. "We need to find another safe house for you and Romi since this location has been breached. They know you're here, and they'll keep coming."

"Tomorrow's Romi's birthday. We're having a small gathering and creek party. She's been excited for weeks. Do you think we can figure out another place to go after that? Maybe add a few guards to be with us tomorrow?"

"We can." He stood and dumped the broken glass into the trash can. "Jake said you can stay on his farm. His place is set up with top-notch security cameras, and we can outfit him with guards."

"Is there anywhere else we can go? I'm not sure moving to his farm is the best idea right now."

"Are you worried because of what happened tonight?"

The image of Jake with his fist in the air flashed through her mind. "I've never seen him like that."

"What do you mean?"

"Don't get me wrong, I'm grateful he stopped the man, but at one point the rage in him scared me."

"Did you say something to him? What made him stop?"

She shook her head. "I only saw one blow.

Jake had the man on the ground. He'd raised his fist to hit him again, then paused in midair. Something snapped him back to reality, but it wasn't me."

Zain stood and handed her back the dustpan. "When Jake loves someone, he'll do whatever it takes to keep them safe. Granted, he went a little too far tonight. Once he had the guy on the ground, he should've cuffed him, then let him be."

Her chest tightened at the word *love*. The Jake she'd witnessed tonight operated from something darker than his love for her. She didn't want to be the one to put him in another situation where he might lose control again. "Maybe it would be best to assign another officer as our guard."

"Then I guess your answer to his invitation is no?"

She stopped sweeping. "I have to think about Romi. Maybe we could find an alternative place to stay."

Zain nodded. "I'll let him know."

"I'd rather tell him if that's okay. He's coming to Romi's birthday party tomorrow. I'll talk to him then."

Skye glanced at the clock on the wall. "I better try to get some sleep if I'm going to be all sunshine and birthday candles for my daughter by noon. See ya at the party?"

"Carli and I will be there."

"Thanks, Zain."

Skye walked to the door, her thoughts still on Jake, wondering where he'd gone for the night. They both needed a break from the case—and maybe from each other. Jake's determination to keep them safe seemed to bring out a dark side of his personality, a side she didn't want around her daughter.

FIFTEEN

Pink polka-dotted balloons swayed in the gentle breeze outside on the back patio as Skye secured the edge of the Happy Birthday banner to the trellis post. Scents of birthday cake and chocolate drifted from the kitchen, where Carli iced Romi's favorite dessert. Skye's daughter ran outside, wearing her new swimsuit and floaties. The little girl loved to swim in the creek.

"Is it time to go swimming yet, Momma?"

Skye stepped off the stool. "Not yet. We still need to set out a few chairs and get the drinks poured. As soon as Eli is ready and a few more guests arrive, we'll go to the swimming hole."

Her daughter's green eyes bubbled with excitement. "I can't wait. I love to go swimming."

Skye pulled her daughter's unruly mane into a cute bundle on top of her head. "Now you really are ready."

"Me, too." Carli's nephew, Eli, came around the corner carrying a blue inner tube and goggles. "I'm going to float from the bridge down to the swimming hole."

"I want to float, too."

"Then go get your pink ring," Skye told her daughter. Romi ran back toward her room with Eli following after her. "Make sure you get it blown up good."

The two of them made quite the pair, and Skye loved every minute with them.

"Whoa. Slow down." Carli carried the cake onto the terrace as the kids ran past her through the door. She placed the dessert onto the picnic table covered with a pink plaid cloth. "I love watching them interact together. Eli thinks he's her big brother and must look out for her."

"I wouldn't have it any other way." Skye leaned over the cake and inhaled. "That smells delicious."

"And it is. There's also a chocolate pudding layer inside."

"Yum. I can't wait to taste a piece." Skye glanced at her watch. The hands displayed fifteen minutes after the designated start time. "Jake should've been here by now. He knew the party started at noon with cake and ice cream to follow. I wonder what's keeping him?"

"Maybe he got tied up with work."

"On a Saturday?"

Zain stepped onto the patio with Cale Hudson, Skye's supervisor, in tow. "I found this guy roaming around out front, looking for a party."

Skye moved across the room to greet him, and Cale handed her a present. "I can't stay but wanted to drop this off for Romi. Turning five is a big deal."

"Thank you so much."

Cale motioned for her to follow him off to the side. "There's one more thing I wanted to talk to you about, and I hate to discuss this today, but it can't wait."

Skyc glanced back at Carli and Zain, who disappeared into the kitchen. "No worries. What's up?"

Cale towered above her and ran a hand through his dark hair. "One of the detectives I spoke with when Penny was arrested keeps calling and asking about our workers. He even came by one time during a workday to 'follow up' on everything. Do you think you could encourage him to give us some space? I don't mind cooperating, but his frequent emails and phone calls are starting to make the drivers antsy."

"Do you mean Jake?"

"I think it's the other one—Nate Steele. We've proven we had no knowledge of the drugs in the shipments, and I'd like the disruptions to our workdays to stop."

"You know, this is more than a drug investigation. They think Randy's murder is tied to all of this."

Cale raised his bushy eyebrows. "Wasn't Randy killed in a car accident?"

"That's what we thought at first, but new evidence shows there was foul play. They think he was killed because of a case he was working on."

His hand brushed her arm. "I'm so sorry. I guess that's why you extended your leave."

"I didn't want to alarm anyone with the details, so I appreciate you approving my request without much explanation."

"We've worked together for years, and I knew you had a good reason. I do hope you'll be able to return soon. The place runs much smoother when you're there."

Skye appreciated the compliment, but she often wondered if there was an ulterior motive behind Cale's remarks. His past history and career ambitions didn't make him a favorite with some of his employees, although she'd always liked working for the man.

"Thank you so much. I hope to be back soon also."

Cale stepped toward the patio screen door. "I really must be going. I hope you have a great party."

She waved goodbye and placed his present on the table for Romi to open later.

Zain walked back into the area, carrying more

food, and glanced at her. "Are we ready to go wading in the creek?"

"Eli and Romi went to get her float. They want to tube from the bridge down to the swimming hole."

"Sounds like fun. Is Jake here yet?"

Skye shook her head. "Did a case or something come up at work?"

"Not that I know of. The other officers wrapped up the paperwork from the incident last night." Zain tapped his phone. "I'll call and see if he's on his way."

After three tries and a couple of voice mails, Zain led their group to the creek. Romi and Eli splashed and skipped rocks. Zain tubed with them from the bridge to the swimming hole while Skye and Carli soaked up the sun on the pebbled bank. Her gaze kept drifting across the field in hopes of Jake showing, but he never arrived.

Carli stood and folded up her chair. She pointed up stream from their location to the dilapidated shelter positioned at the top of the bank. "Goodness, I need to tell Zain to tear the old picnic shed down. That's so dangerous, especially with the kids getting older. With one more storm, that thing could fall into the creek."

"So true." Skye stood and collected the toys around them, placing them in her swim bag. "I'm still concerned about Jake. He promised he'd be here. He even told me he had a present for Romi. Did he ever return Zain's call?"

Carli reached into her bag and retrieved Zain's phone. "Let me check." She tapped the screen. "Looks like he texted him. He's not coming. Said something came up."

"I hope everything's okay."

"I'm sure he has a good explanation."

"Yeah, like he decided to bail on the girl who friend zoned him. Maybe I messed up, Carli. I never should've given an ultimatum. He said he wanted more, but I pushed for a commitment. We haven't seen each other in seven years, and after how things ended last time, how could I expect him to take such a large step?"

Carli folded up the plastic-backed blanket and slipped it into her bag. "You and Jake have danced around each other for too long, except for your time with Randy. You have a daughter to consider, and if Jake can't understand your need for a commitment after his history, then the best thing to do is let him go."

"I wish he was easy to let go." Skye reached for a towel, glancing up the river when her daughter squealed, riding the tube toward them. "You're right about one thing."

"What's that?"

Skye nodded toward the dilapidated shelter. "That shed definitely needs to come down."

Romi hopped out of the tube and walked up

onto the pebbled bank. Skye removed her life vest and wrapped her daughter in the towel. "Are you ready to go back to the house, eat cake and open presents?"

Romi jumped up and down, her lips lined with a slight hint of blue from the cold water. "Yes, yes, yes."

They returned to the house, grilled some burgers and Skye let Romi enjoy the rest of her birthday, pushing all thoughts of Jake to the side. Her little girl would only turn five once, and Skye refused to let anyone cloud the moment.

Romi ran from one toy to another, unsure of which to play with first, while Skye collected empty plates and cups, returning them to the hot, sudsy water in the kitchen sink. Carli followed her inside.

"Are you sure you're going to be okay?" her friend asked.

Skye grabbed a sponge, dunked her hands into the warm water and scrubbed one of the plates. "I'm fine. Today is Romi's day, and even though I can't believe he didn't come, I'm not going to let his absence keep me from soaking up every moment."

"Maybe there's an explanation as to why he decided not to be here. Is his mother okay?"

Her scrubbing slowed. "I didn't think about that. You don't suppose something happened to her, do you?"

Carli dried a plate and placed it in the cabinet. "He probably would've mentioned something in his text if his reason involved her. My guess is he's rethinking his actions last night and feels ashamed about how he acted. He's probably too embarrassed to show up today."

"I admit he scared me, but the intruder planned to kill us. Sure, Jake went a little overboard, but he saved our lives, and I'll always be indebted to him."

"Maybe you need to tell him. If he's worried about being around you and Romi, then some encouragement could ease his mind. The only way the two of you move forward is if you talk. I'm happy to stay with the kids if you want."

"I should stay and finish cleaning up."

"The dishwasher's loaded and I'm planning to fix a large pot of spaghetti for supper later, which is Romi's favorite. She's so busy playing with her toys and Eli, she won't even notice you're gone." Carli lifted her keys from a hook. "Here, take my car."

Skye pulled her hands from the water and dried them with a paper towel. "Maybe I should go check on him and make sure his mom's okay. I won't be long. I know I'll feel better if I can talk to him about everything that happened last night."

"Go. Romi keeps Eli entertained, which is a

win for me and Zain. The boy has been super clingy lately. He misses his father."

Skye grabbed her bag from the chair. "When's Tyler supposed to be back?"

"He has a break coming up. I can't believe my brother decided to become a US Marshal instead of going to law school."

"I bet you'll be glad to have him home for a while."

"I will, and so will Eli."

"Well, five months will go by fast and then Tyler will have his dream career, like he's always wanted." Skye motioned to the kids. "You sure you don't mind watching her?"

"Not at all. She's precious."

"Thanks again, Carli. I'd be a mess if I didn't have you."

With a quick hug, Skye headed out the door and drove to Jake's farm. His paved driveway wound back into the trees, then opened up to a large swath of land. She barely remembered the place. They hadn't spent much time at his home when they were younger. Jake never wanted any of his friends around his father and only invited them over if the man was away.

Far from the chipped gray paint and over-grown landscaping of the past, his refurbished house boasted white siding and a great room addition, with large windows overlooking his vast amount of pastureland.

Skye parked behind a small silver sedan and made her way to the front door.

Nerves tingled through her body. She hadn't planned what to say, but she knew they had to talk so she could make sure he was okay.

Skye pressed the bell and waited. The door swung open, but instead of Jake standing on the other side, his mother greeted her with a curious smile.

"Ms. Reed. I'm not sure you remember me." She held out her hand. "I'm Skye Anderson."

The petite lady with white hair and kind eyes took Skye's hand and pulled her into a hug. "Of course, I remember you. You were always my favorite friend of Jake's. Come in and have some tea with me on the back patio."

Skye followed the woman inside, admiring the Southern charm decor and brightness of the remodel. Evening light spilled through large windows and soft gray walls stood as backdrops for art pieces made and signed by local artists. "Did you do the interior decorating?"

"Heavens, no. Jake has quite the eye for detail. You should see some of the furniture pieces he's made. They're simply stunning."

"Jake makes furniture?"

"He works on his designs after every shift. Says the projects help him relax and let go of the day's horrors. I guess homicide detectives see more than their share of evil. He's working on an old antique dresser of mine right now and wants to fix the back piece that was broken many years ago."

"Is he in his workshop? I'd really like to talk with him."

Ms. Reed lifted the tea pitcher and poured two glasses, offering one to Skye. "He left earlier this morning and said he had a meeting he needed to attend, but he didn't tell me where. Or maybe he did but I don't remember. I hope he gets back before dark. I still worry about him like he was a kid." She pointed to the backyard. "Would you like to walk through my gardens? That's my place of serenity."

Jake's mother had won awards for her prized flowers, and she didn't let just anyone venture into her meticulously cultivated arboretum.

"I'd be honored." Skye followed her through the French patio doors.

They meandered through the curved pathways of the backyard while Ms. Reed shared a little about each flower, but then she stopped at the roses. "Most people put roses on a pedestal, but while they are beautiful, I always hated the thorns. Pricked me every time."

"What's your favorite flower?"

The older woman walked to an area of wildflowers and picked a small yellow one. "The buttercup. It's small and simple, like me, I suppose. When my sisters and I were teenagers, we used to pick them and hold them under each other's chins. If we saw yellow, we knew they liked a boy and we would tease them relentlessly." She let out a giggle. "Oh, how we would tease."

"But I always heard when a person saw the gold reflection on their skin, it meant they liked butter."

"Well, that was too boring for my sisters and me. This was our way of getting one another to spill their secret crushes."

"Did you tell them yours?"

Her shoulders dipped. "I did. Jake's father always held my heart from the first day we met. At one time, he was a lovely man, took such good care of us, but when the police force let him go, he turned to alcohol and his whole demeanor changed. Jake often took the brunt of his father's outbursts. I tried to leave with Jake several times, but his father always found us and brought us back. Had it not been for God bringing Randy and his parents into our lives, I'm not sure where we would be."

"I miss Randy's parents so much. Romi does, too, but at least we get to visit them each year in Florida over Christmas break, or they come up to see us."

"And what about your parents?"

"My mom left when I was twelve, and after a few tries to reconnect with a woman who no longer wanted a relationship with her daughter,

I gave up. Dad died a few years ago from heart issues."

"I'm so sorry."

"That's why I remain close to my in-laws. I want Romi to know her grandparents. She loves swimming in their pool."

"Sounds like your little girl has quite a blessed life." She walked a little farther, twirling the buttercup between her fingers. "I'm actually glad you stopped by. Jake came home the other night pretty upset, but he didn't want to talk about what happened. Do you have any idea what's going on with him?"

Skye glanced toward a birdbath, where a yellow finch doused his wings. "We had an intruder at the ranch house, and Jake saved my life."

"That doesn't sound like something he needs to be upset over."

"The intruder fought with Jake, and I think after he put the guy down, the incident reminded him of his last encounter with his father."

"Hmm. He's nothing like his father, you know."

Skye tried to reconcile her words with the images still fresh in her mind. "I don't really remember too much about Jake's dad, but if Jake hadn't been at the house, I'm scared to think of what would've happened."

"A crying shame these evil people are trying to hurt you and Romi. If I know Jake, he'll do everything in his power to stop them. Sometimes the actions he takes on the job give him the notion he's no different than his father. I try to tell him the truth, but I can't seem to get through to him. I hope you can."

"Me? I think I'm the last person he'll listen to right now."

Ms. Reed twirled the buttercup again. "Oh, my dear, he'll listen to you more than you know." She held the flower underneath Skye's chin and let the petals tickle her skin. "Interesting…you like a boy, too."

Skye did like Jake, more than she wanted, but they'd never had a problem with attraction and chemistry. Their issues diverged when life's struggles got in the way. They both wanted something different for their futures.

Ms. Reed creaked open a wooden gate at the back of the property and led her to a one-room block building painted gray. The windows held boxes of colorful flowers, and the wooden door was painted teal.

Jake's mother placed her wrinkled hand on the doorknob and pointed to the flowers. "I dressed up the outside for him a little."

She pressed the door open and pulled a chain, turning on a light. Dust floated through the air, and a faint glow from the setting sun filtered through the window. The smell of sawdust filled the space, and scraps of wood littered the floor around a beautiful antique dresser seated in the middle of the room.

"Is this the piece Jake's repairing for you?" Skye asked.

"Sure is. Isn't it beautiful? My great-grandmother gave the dresser to my grandmother and my grandmother to my mother and then to me. He only has one more sanding and a final coat of sealer, then it will be finished."

Skye ran her fingers over the smoothed wood grain Jake's hands had restored. "I never knew he was so talented."

"I'm not."

Both women spun around at Jake's voice. He stood in the doorway, his hands folded across his chest.

He shot a glance toward his mother, then refocused on Skye. "I didn't know you planned to come by."

His words seemed tense and heat rushed to her face. "When you didn't show for Romi's party, I wanted to see if you were okay. Your mom was showing me around. I love all the improvements you've made to the place. The house and gardens are beautiful."

He let his gaze linger on her for a moment, and she shifted her weight underneath his observation. "Good to hear. Should make the place easier to sell."

Ms. Reed straightened at his statement. "What

are you talking about? We're not selling this place."

"Mom, we'll talk later about this. Right now, Skye, if you don't mind, I'll walk you to your car."

She dusted her hands against her jeans and gave Ms. Reed a quick thank-you, then moved past Jake into the night air. Lightning bugs danced through the field in front of her, elusive and out of reach. Similar to the man still inside.

Jake removed the tarp covering the wooden rocking horse he'd made for Romi and carried the gift onto the patio. Skye stood with her back to him, staring at the dark field beyond his front yard. She turned, folded her arms across her chest. Her gaze dropped to the rocking horse he'd made, but she remained quiet.

"This is for Romi. Do you mind giving it to her for me?"

"You should be the one to give her the gift. She asked for you today at her birthday party. I told her you would be there."

He hated to disappoint Randy's daughter on her birthday, but with his decision to move, he didn't want to make his absence any harder. "Under the circumstances, I think the gift would come best from you."

Skye dropped her arms and took a step toward him. "Jake, what's going on?"

"The man who broke into the safe house escaped from the hospital early this morning. A transport tech took him for his scheduled brain scan, and the man never returned. The officer who escorted him down got jumped in a back hallway by a couple of thugs, all with skull tattoos on their arms."

"That's not good."

He motioned toward her car, his latest decision weighing heavy on his mind. "I'm sure he'll come after me once his injuries heal, and I can't let him get near you and Romi. I won't put the two of you in any more danger than I already have."

"You've kept danger *from* us."

"The attacks on your life didn't start until I reopened the case. I'm the one who upended your life in a selfish pursuit of Randy's killer."

"Your decision wasn't selfish—"

He held up his hand. "I'm moving back to Charlotte. I went for a meeting today. I can redirect Carello's attention to me and off you by running a task force with ops to make him forget all about you. I start in a couple of weeks. I think you have the right idea about witness protection, at least until we have Dante behind bars."

"I can't believe you're leaving us, right when we need you most."

"After last night, I'm only making things worse."

"That's not true. You kept us safe."

"You're not safe. My inability to control my temper only put you in more danger. Zain's right—my decisions lately have been reckless and fueled by vengeance. The only way for me to make things right is to leave. Zain's team will do everything to keep you safe until the investigation closes, but I'm no longer a part of the group."

"But you're the only one I trust. You can't leave again. Not when I just got you back."

Her words stabbed at his soul. He loved her, but sometimes a person had to let go of the things he loved. "I never meant to hurt you, Skye."

She stepped close to him. "Leaving hurts me. You, not in my life, hurts me. Please, don't go. I know I told you we couldn't be together, but Romi loves having you around, and we can figure out a way to make this work. I'm willing to be flexible, not place any demands on you. But you can't go."

Jake shook his head, picked up the rocking horse again and slid the gift into her back seat. "I'm sorry, but I've made up my mind. This is what's best for you."

"Then we'll come with you. I'll transfer to the Charlotte post office. With the Charlotte PD looking out for us, Carello will stay away."

"I don't want you there, Skye." His words snapped sharper than he wanted, but if being harsh kept her safe, then so be it. The pain he inflicted glistened in her eyes and sent an ache through his chest. She said nothing.

Jake's phone rang, interrupting the moment, and Zain's name lit up the screen. "Reed here."

"Looks like we've had another breach in security here at the ranch. One of the guards saw a man at the edge of the property skulking around. I need all hands over here until we can find him."

"I'm on my way." Jake ended the call and barely glanced at her. "I've got to go. Another intruder's on the property at the ranch. I need to head over there to help them find the man. You should stay here with Mom until everything's been cleared."

Skye grabbed her keys from her purse, opened the driver's side door and tossed her bag inside. "My daughter's there, and I'm tired of everyone telling me what I should and shouldn't do. If Carello wants me dead, then let him come at me head-on."

"It's too dangerous. I'm sure Zain has Romi well secured."

She swiped the wetness from her cheeks. "Jake, you've made it clear you don't want me in your life, therefore you have no right to tell me what to do. I'm going."

She slid into the driver's seat, started Carli's car, and rolled down her window. "Do you want to follow me or am I following you?"

He stared, trying to think of a way to convince

her otherwise, but he'd seen that look in her eye before. "Follow me."

Jake jogged to his car, slipped it into Drive, then glanced in his rearview mirror. Skye moved in behind him, the glow of her headlights close. Maybe he was making a mistake by leaving, but they'd had their chance a long time ago. His actions from the other night had put her and Romi in more danger, and the only action left to take was to keep Skye far from Carello's men when they came for revenge.

SIXTEEN

Skye parked Carli's car in front of the guest-house and ran up to her room. She opened the closet, reached for the locked gun safe on the top shelf, then placed her fingertip against the scanner. The lid popped open, and she removed her Glock 19 from the case, checking the magazine for bullets. She clicked the safety off, headed downstairs and back across the field to the main house.

Jake stood in the kitchen with Zain and several other officers. A large topographical map of the ranch stretched across the kitchen table. His gaze found hers when she entered, then dropped to the gun in her hand. She shoved it into the back of her pants and joined them.

Zain pointed to the area bordering Crystal Creek. "Jake, you take this zone near the covered bridge over to the road. That should be the last piece of the property to search."

"What about me?" Skye asked. "Where do you want me to search?"

Zain shot a look at Jake. "I want you to stay here with Carli and the kids where you'll be safe."

Her heart longed to stay with her daughter, but if she and Romi were ever going to have a normal life again, this man needed to be found, and she planned to help. "I know this property like the back of my hand. Let me join the search. I can't sit still and wait anymore."

"Fine. Pair up with Jake." Zain motioned to the door. "Let's go."

Everyone exited the guesthouse and walked toward the fields. Hundreds of yards passed before Skye reached their assigned quadrant, lined up along the edge near the property line. She retrieved her weapon and racked the slide. Jake joined her and glanced at her hand again. "Don't shoot unless I tell you to."

She gripped her gun tighter. "I'm a responsible, trained gun owner, Jake. I know whether or not to shoot."

His expression softened. "I know you do, but we want this guy alive. We need him to answer our questions, and after your last target practice on the truck grille, this guy doesn't have a chance if you take a shot."

She pressed her lips together to keep from smiling. Her shooting skills had impressed him, and they should. She'd taken out all three lights with little effort. If needed, she'd do the same to the man terrorizing her and her daughter.

Zain's voice sounded through the police radio clipped to Jake's belt. "Move out."

At least thirty officers stalked across the fields and into the woods past the large barns on the property. Jake and Skye followed suit.

Cicadas chirped, surrounding them with their summer song. More lightning bugs danced between the trees as if all were well despite the threats looming in the shadows. The air smelled of rain and carried a low rumble of thunder in the distance.

"Your mom doesn't seem like she wants to move to Charlotte."

"She will after I have a chance to talk to her about the job. I can't leave her here alone. She'll mess up her medicine again and end up back in the hospital."

Skye stepped over a dead log lying in her path. She liked Jake's mother. She was sweet, and without a mother figure of her own nearby, she wanted to help. "You know, I could stop by in the mornings on my way to work and make sure she takes the correct medications. After all these years, I hate to see her have to give up her home."

He stopped walking and faced her. "You'd do that for her?"

"Of course. Randy's parents are in Florida, and I miss having an older, wiser person's perspective sometimes. I'd be happy to help through the week."

He restarted his trek. "You're sweet, but I can't expect you to disrupt your life for my mother. She'll be fine with me."

Skye held up her hands. "Just throwing the option out there. She didn't seem too happy about your choice."

"Something the two of you have in common."

Jake stopped again and held up his fist, a universal sign to freeze all motion—a gesture Randy had taught her when they were dating.

The snap of a twig to the right redirected their attention. Skye aimed her weapon, searching for their suspect. Moonbeams streaked through the wooded canopy, casting a dim glow.

Do you see anything?"

"Nothing."

They took another step.

One lone gunshot echoed across the terrain. Jake and Skye dropped low behind a tree, and he scanned the area with his night-vision goggles.

"Sounded like the shot came from the right, down near the creek," she said.

"There's no one on our right side. We're at the edge of the property. All the other officers are searching to our left."

"Do you think it was a neighbor or a hunter?"

"Maybe. Let's keep moving. Stay low. The last thing we want is for the suspect to get a jump on us."

They started out again, moving at a swifter pace, checking for anything out of the ordinary. Water rushed up ahead, and the covered bridge rose in front of them. Jake took a seat on the ground and scanned the bank.

Skye tapped his arm. "Can I take a look?"

He handed her the goggles. "Wonder if anybody else has found him yet? I'd like to know this guy is in custody before the night's over."

She searched along the creek bank and under the bridge as far as she could see. "I don't think anyone's found him yet. Zain would've radioed." Skye handed back the goggles. "Look underneath the bridge, on the opposite edge of the riverbank."

Jake pressed the device to his eyes and turned the focus. "There's a man down there."

"Crumpled on the ground, not moving. You think he's our security breach?"

"Only one way to find out."

They shuffled down the bank and stopped at the edge of the water. The man faced away from them, his body lying on his left side.

Jake stepped into the water. "I want to make sure he's our guy."

Skye stood back, her weapon aimed at the body in case the man revived and became violent. She waited as Jake crossed the river, the water cresting to his knees. Once out the other side, he knelt next to the body, blocking her view.

"No. It can't be."

"What?" Skye started across for a better angle. Jake shoved his gun in his holster, then ripped off his outer shirt, wadded the garment into a ball and pressed the material to the man's abdomen.

"Jake, who is it?"

"My dad. Hurry and get someone else down here."

"Your dad?" Skye picked up her pace, climbing out of the water beside him. He handed her his radio.

"Call for backup and get me an ambulance here. His pulse is weak, but he's still alive."

Skye pressed the side button. "We've got a victim on the ground and need an ambulance in zone 12 near the bridge."

A tone chirped when she released her finger.

Zain's voice filtered through. "Are y'all okay? We heard the gunshot and are moving in your direction."

"We're fine. The man who was shot is Jake's father, and he's still alive but needs medical attention."

"We're on our way."

Skye clipped the radio back on his belt and stared at the unconscious man. His dad hadn't darkened the door of Crystal Creek in years. "Do you know why he's here?" she asked.

"Not a clue."

Skye wasn't sure how Jake's father fit into all this, but someone had decided to stop the old man from returning—or maybe this was retaliation for Jake's fight and arrest of one of Carello's members.

Cream-colored tile stretched across the floor of the hospital's waiting room, and with every click of the surgical suite doors, Jake glanced up. His father's operation to remove the bullet in his abdomen was stretching on for hours.

He paced back and forth from the vending machines to the vinyl chairs meant to provide a comfortable place to sit. He hoped someone would tell him something soon. Questions rattled around in his brain after finding his father shot and left for dead on the creek bank after nine years of no contact.

"Why don't you sit down? The surgeon will tell you something as soon as he can." Skye motioned toward the seat next to her.

Jake lowered himself into the chair again. "I can't believe he's back. What was he doing at the ranch?"

"I don't know, but when he gets out of surgery, we can ask him. Did you call your mom and tell her?"

He shook his head. "I don't want her anywhere near him until I understand why he's here."

The department doors swung open, and the trauma surgeon emerged. "Are you with Mr. Reed?"

"I'm his son," Jake said.

"Great. His records indicate you have permission for us to discuss his medical condition with you. He's out of surgery, and the procedure went well. We were able to extract the bullet, remove his spleen and repair the large intestine. We'll need to watch him closely for the next few days for infection."

"How long will he be in the hospital?"

"The next twenty-four hours will tell us more, but I'm hoping if all goes well, no more than a few days. Then he'll need rehab to rebuild strength in his core muscles, and he may need to be in a wheelchair for a while until he can stand and walk again on his own. Most of all, he's going to need his family to help him."

Jake struggled with the idea of providing support for the man who had caused so much trauma in their lives. He decided not to share his brutal past with the doctor.

Instead, Jake wanted answers. "May we see him?"

"Absolutely. He's been admitted to room 378."

Jake started down the hall toward his father's

room, and Skye fell in step beside him, placing a hand on his arm.

"Hold up for a minute."

He slowed his steps.

"You haven't seen this man in nine years. You can't storm in there and expect answers. Do you have a plan before you walk into his room?"

"Not really, other than asking him why's he back and does he know who shot him? There's got to be a reason for his return."

"And we'll find out his reason, but remember, even though things didn't end well between the two of you…he's still your father."

Jake ran a hand through his hair. "Don't remind me."

She placed her hand in his and Jake straightened, knocking on door 378. He pushed the barrier open and, for the first time in years, his gaze rested on the man he used to call Dad.

A silvery-gray scruff lined his father's jaw, accentuating the sallowness of his cheeks. He looked smaller than Jake remembered, and thinner, but his expression brightened when they entered the room.

"I didn't think you'd come."

Jake didn't want to give his father the wrong impression. "I'm only here to ask you some questions about your shooting. I'm hoping you can help us identify who did this to you."

His dad's gaze shifted past him. "Who's with you? Is that Skye?"

"Yes, Mr. Reed. You gave us quite a scare."

"Doc says I'm gonna be okay as long as I do exactly what he says."

Jake leaned against the wall opposite his dad's bed. "Do you remember being at the ranch tonight?"

"Of course, I do. I came to give you a message."

"A message? From whom?"

"Dante Carello."

Jake caught the look Skye shot him from across the room. "How do you know Dante?"

"I opened a private investigator office in a neighboring county, and Dante came by one day. He hired me to look into an old case the police had filed as an accident."

Jake straightened with his news. He didn't realize his father had been so close all this time. "If you're talking about Randy's case, I've been looking into his death."

His father lifted a remote and inclined the back of his bed a bit more, grimacing through the pain. "You got Randy's file? I wasn't sure if you had."

"*You* left the file for me?"

"Yeah. When I started investigating Lorna's death, I came across Randy's investigation and tried to meet with him. He refused to see me.

Didn't want anything to do with someone working with Dante. I followed Randy on a couple of occasions, hoping to get a moment to speak with him tell him what I uncovered." His dad's gaze shifted to Skye. "I saw what happened the night he died."

She took a step closer to the old man's bed. "You saw who killed Randy?"

"I couldn't see the man's face from my line of vision, but I saw him stab Randy in the neck. I tried to tell the cops at the precinct what really happened, but no one listened. You'd think completing rehab and nine years of sobriety would count for something."

Jake noticed his father's hopeful gaze but gave him no response.

"Anyway, I had a friend who was a judge and he gave me a court order for Randy's accident report and medical files. Randy and Lorna had the same knife slits to the throat. The officers dismissed hers as an injury from the fall, and they dismissed your husband's as an injury from the wreck. But both victims had two-inch serrated cuts to their left carotid artery, most likely made by the same knife."

Jake shook his head. "Lorna died more than ten years ago. Why would her death have anything to do with Randy's?"

"Randy found out that Dante Carello and Lorna had a big fight and broke up the night of her death. Apparently, they were planning to get married. At first Randy's notes indicated Dante may have pushed Lorna during a lovers' argument, but Carello had an alibi."

Jake moved into the recliner positioned next to his father's bed. "He could've sent one of his thugs to do his dirty work, like he's done with Skye. The skull tattoos are tied to Carello's gang, and every one of her attackers have had one on their forearm."

"I asked Dante about them. He said about six months before Randy died, several of his members went rogue, working for someone else, but he never was able to figure out who. He thinks they're the ones behind Skye's attacks."

"Well, isn't that convenient?" Jake said. "What makes more sense is that he had someone kill his girlfriend when she dumped him and then he offed Randy when he discovered who killed Lorna."

His father placed an ice chip into his mouth. "I don't think so. The man has been searching for her killer ever since she died. He wants to meet with you and Skye, to talk about what she saw the night of the accident. I was on my way to set up a meeting with you when someone shot me as I crossed the bridge. I hear they stole my car and left me for dead."

"Wait. You're telling me Dante Carello wants Skye alive?" Jake asked.

"She's the only other person who lost a loved one, same as Dante, and rumor has it she's remembered more about the killer than anyone else, so yes, he wants her alive."

Skye leaned against the wall. "Then who's been trying to kill me all this time?"

Jake's father shrugged. "Probably the man who killed Lorna, your husband and almost killed me."

Blue lights still flashed around the main house, although hours had passed since they'd found Jake's dad. The investigation must be taking longer than expected. Skye stepped from the SUV, still trying to determine if the man was lying for Dante or telling them the truth.

Jake touched her arm. "Before we go inside, I wanted to tell you I've decided to stay until we find the person behind Randy and Lorna's deaths."

"You think what your father said is true?"

"My father might've done some evil things, but he wasn't a liar, and when he was sober, he was a great detective."

"Like father, like son."

Jake shoved his hands in his pockets and shrugged. "In more ways than one, I guess."

"Hey." She stepped closer, letting her hands rest on his arms. "You're not your father. You're one of the kindest, most thoughtful men I know, and you're an amazing detective. We're going to figure this out, together."

His shoulders lifted with her words, and he motioned toward the front door of Zain and Carli's house. "Shall we go share everything we've learned tonight about our case?"

"I'll leave the revelation up to you. I just want to hold my daughter."

They walked up the steps, and the door swung open. Zain stood in the opening with Carli behind him in tears. "Did you get my calls?"

Jake pulled out his phone and shook his head. "Looks like my phone's dead. We've been at the hospital, and I didn't even notice—"

"Romi's gone." Carli wiped a tissue under her eyes.

"What?" Skye said and clutched Jake's arm.

"Romi's missing. She and Eli were in the den watching cartoons, and I went into the kitchen for one moment to get them some popcorn and juice. When I came back, Eli was in the adjoining bathroom and Romi was missing. We searched the whole house, thinking she might be playing hide-and-seek like earlier, but they always use a safe word, 'puppy,' when they get tired of looking, but she never—"

Carli's voice choked with sobs.

Skye pushed past them both and rushed into the living room. "Romi?"

The stuffed horse Jake had given her daughter

rested on the carpet beside a pink toddler chair. She'd never leave without taking her toy. Skye knelt to the floor and clutched the stuffed animal to her chest.

SEVENTEEN

Skye stood next to Jake and told him to reverse the security footage from the camera and play the frames again. "There." She pointed. "See the shadow at the edge of the patio? Romi walks outside when the shadow emerges."

"Yeah. Can you tell who that is?" Jake zoomed up the darker area and slowed down the speed.

"I can't see their face, but they're on a side-by-side."

"Which means there won't be a scent for Sully to trace."

"Wait. Romi's saying something to them, then she runs back inside. What is she doing?"

Skye's daughter returned with her floaties on her arms and climbed into the seat.

"The only reason she would've gotten her floaties would be to go to the creek."

"Then we need to get down there." Jake stood from the desk. "Search the banks. Maybe they're still there."

Intense panic sheared every nerve inside Skye's body. This was her worst nightmare. She should've been there, should have kept her daughter by her side. What kind of mother left her kid with a friend when there was a killer on the property? She couldn't change the fact Romi had been taken, but she could hustle to find her.

God, please protect my daughter.

Lightning flashed across the sky, and a low rumble of thunder warned of an impending storm. Skye slid beside Jake into a side-by-side vehicle, while Carli and Zain followed in a truck.

Rain pelted down on the metal roof, but they raced toward the creek bank near her daughter's favorite tubing spot. Skye pointed to a rocky beach where she and Romi liked to skip stones. "Let me check the shore."

Jake swerved in that direction and stopped the vehicle. The group jumped out and fanned across the area, ignoring the immediate soaking they received from the rain.

Skye slid down the bank first. "Romi?"

The little girl didn't answer. Clouds covering the moon darkened the area more than normal. Jake swept his flashlight across the landscape. The rain intensified.

Skye yelled again. "Romi?"

Still no answer. Her friends' voices echoed in the distance, all of them searching for her little girl.

Skye climbed over the rocks, which were slippery from the weather, and searched behind every boulder along the twenty-foot stretch. Her daughter wasn't there. "I thought for sure she'd come here. This is where she always wants to play."

"We'll find her." Jake flashed the light up and down each side of the creek bed, illuminating streaks of rain from above.

"Let's move on down." Skye walked halfway back up the bank and then stopped. "Do you hear that?"

Jake straightened, aiming his light toward the sound. Tall trees draped in kudzu waved in the wind and brushed the sides of the old picnic shed overhanging the creek below.

"Someone's crying. It's coming from over there, near the old structure on the left," Skye said, scrambling closer. "Romi?"

The little girl's head popped up from one of the benches. "Mommy?"

Skye rushed into the structure. The rotten boards creaked and bent under her weight. Several planks were missing, providing a view of the white water below. One wrong step and Skye or Romi might be swept away in the strong current. "Don't move, baby. I'm going to get you. Stay really still, okay?"

Romi sniffled. "Okay."

Jake ran up behind her. "Those boards are rotten. If we step on them—"

"How'd they get her over there? This shed is wide. How did they keep from falling through when they put her on the bench?"

"Maybe they forced her to walk over there alone. I'll go get her."

Jake stepped back toward the ATV, leaving Skye feeling nauseous at the idea of her daughter being forced to cross the rotting structure. If she ever got her hands on these people, she feared she would do much worse than Jake's actions from the other night.

"Mr. Jake's going to come get you, Romi. You sit really still for me, okay?"

Her daughter nodded.

He returned with a rope in his hand, and Skye pointed to the ceiling joists. "Maybe they're still solid."

"My thoughts exactly. I'll toss the rope over them and create a harness on this end. Can you support us on this side?"

"I'll do whatever is needed."

Jake climbed up on one of the solid railings and threaded the line across the horizontal beam, then made a harness with multiple knots to secure his weight.

"Where'd you learn how to do that?"

"I used to rappel with a bunch of guys from the Charlotte department."

"Be careful."

Skye stood to the side and wrapped her end of the rope around one of the more solid posts. Jake walked along the center floor joist, placing one foot in front of the other, while Romi stared at him.

He took another step closer. The board beneath him cracked but didn't break. Skye pulled on the rope to lift him. Another set of hands grabbed the rope behind her and pulled, lifting Jake on his tiptoes. She turned.

Zain stood by her side. "We've got them."

With a few more steps, Jake reached for Romi's hand. His fingers brushed hers. "Okay, sweet girl. Be really careful and stand up on the bench for me."

Skye's daughter followed Jake's instructions.

"Now, on three, I want you to take a big leap into my arms. Okay?"

Romi nodded, her eyes wide with fear.

"One, two, three."

She jumped and landed in Jake's arms while Zain and Skye pulled the other end of the rope for support. A loud pop shot through the air, and the rope went slack. The ceiling beam snapped with the extra weight, and Jake fell through the floor with Romi still in his arms. Skye released the rope and scrambled to the edge of the jagged opening in the floor.

"Romi!"

Jake and her daughter splashed into the rushing waters below. The current carried them downstream until the rope caught tight. Zain struggled to hold them.

"Skye, grab the rope and let's pull them over to the bank."

She belly crawled back to solid ground and helped pull against the current of the powerful water. A clash of thunder vibrated the ground, and lightning lit the night.

Romi's pink floaties displayed themselves in the glow. Her daughter's arms clung to Jake's neck as he swam to the edge.

He pulled Romi onto the pebbles, and Skye raced down the bank to gather up her daughter. "You're okay, baby."

The little girl clutched her mother and then pulled back to look at her face. "I got to go swimming."

Skye released a nervous laugh. "Yes, you did."

Jake removed his harness and then collapsed back onto the pebbled beach. "Is she okay?"

Skye reached for his hand. "She's good, thanks to you."

Zain shuffled down the bank toward them, helping them to the top. Skye held Romi, slipped into the ATV and rode with Jake back to the house. Once inside, she wrapped her daughter in a towel and held her close in a recliner, hoping the warmth would stop her daughter's shivers. She snuggled against Skye's chest.

Jake entered the room and pushed the ottoman next to them. He placed his hand on the back of Romi's head and brushed his fingers through her curls. "How's she doing?"

"Still a bit shaken, but okay, I think."

Romi leaned back and put her little hands on Skye's cheeks. "They have Boppi, Mommy."

"What?"

"Boppi, the rabbit Daddy gave me."

Skye shot a worried look at Jake. Romi's toy had been lost since the night of the wreck, and crews had never found the stuffed animal afterward. If the man had Boppi, then the stuffed toy placed him at Randy's murder.

"Who had Boppi?"

"The man who took me for a ride. He said if Mommy stayed quiet, then Boppi and me would be safe."

The threat permeated through Skye. No matter where she hid or how far she ran, Randy's killer could get to her daughter and take her away like they had tonight.

For the first time since Randy's death, Skye regretted helping the police with her husband's case. Her memories wouldn't bring her husband back but remaining silent could keep her daughter alive.

* * *

The next day, Jake carried two suitcases up to the guest apartment located over his attached garage. Skye finally agreed to relocate to Jake's farm. If the decision was up to him, he'd take them out of the state, but with his mom's illness, he wanted to remain close by, especially with his father back in town.

He stood in the bedroom doorway and watched Skye hang a few of Romi's clothes into the closet. Her hair hung down her back, clasped in a tie. She wore little makeup, but in his opinion, she didn't need any.

She turned, caught him staring and placed a hand on her chest. "Goodness. You scared me."

"Sorry. Not my intention." He pointed at the suitcases. "I think that's the last of them."

"I appreciate you bringing them up."

He glanced around the space. "Will this be enough room for you and Romi?"

She motioned to the twin bed where her daughter slept. "Yeah. We don't need much. I think all the late-night trauma exhausted her. Thanks again for letting us stay."

"Of course. I'm glad you're here."

She fiddled with a few of the shirts in the case. "You know they'll find us here, too. Whoever's behind this has some vast resources, and they'll keep hunting me down or threatening my daughter."

"Maybe but changing locations will buy us some time. Zain and I reached out to Dante Carello. He's agreed to meet and share what he knows about Lorna's death. We'll see if any of the info he gives matches to Randy's murder."

"I never thought a drug kingpin would help us find my husband's killer."

"Me neither." Jake stepped toward the door. "By the way, Mom's got some lunch ready in the kitchen, if you're hungry."

"I'll be down in a minute."

He headed back into the main living area. His mom sliced cantaloupe at the kitchen island. Jake popped a piece into his mouth.

"Hey, boy. That's for lunch and our guests."

Footsteps creaked on the stairs from the hallway behind them. Skye escorted a sleepy Romi into the room. The little girl's dark curls coiled in different directions. "Someone woke up hungry."

"No worries." Jake's mom pulled out a stool. "I've got a spot right here and sandwich cubes already made for her."

"Ms. Reed, you didn't have to do all this."

"Nonsense. I had the time. Also, please call me Hanelle or Hani. You're my guest, and there's no sense in formality."

Skye smiled and placed her daughter in the seat. "Thank you, Hanelle. And if you ever need me to fix any food for you or Jake's father during his rehabilitation, I'd be happy to help."

His mother stopped slicing fruit and looked at her son. "Your father?"

In the midst of finding Romi, Jake had neglected to tell his mom about his father's return or hospital stay.

"I haven't had a chance to tell you. There was a shooting at the ranch the other night, and Dad was the victim. He's at the hospital and will probably be there for the rest of the week."

His mother placed her knife on the counter and untied her apron. "Oh my. I should go see him."

"No, Mom. I don't think visiting him is a good idea for you."

Her gaze snapped to his. "And when did you start telling a grown woman what to do? I've been praying for him lately, and this is a God-given opportunity. Plus, I have a few things I want to say to the man."

"He hurt you, and I don't want you around him."

"He's not going to do anything to me while he's lying in a hospital bed with nurses and doctors around." Her face hardened. "I never forgave myself for letting him hurt you, and I have a right to face him now."

"Then let me go with you. I'd feel better knowing I'm there, or at least nearby."

"All right. We can go after dinner tonight. If you don't mind, I'd like a few minutes to myself on the porch." She lifted her glass of iced tea, exited the kitchen, took a seat in her rocker, and bowed her head in prayer. Jake glanced at Skye, unsure of what to say.

He never wanted to talk about his father, and now Jake struggled with the man's reemergence in his life. Sure, his father had gone to rehab and was nine years sober, but one relapse could put his mother back in harm's way.

EIGHTEEN

Skye cleaned up the lunch dishes and stored everything in the fridge while Romi played in the open living area with toy cars. She kept her stuffed horse from Jake in her lap and never let the plush animal go.

Hanelle still rocked in her chair on the back porch, although, Skye noticed, she'd stopped praying.

Jake had vanished to his wood shop, and she hadn't seen him for at least an hour. Maybe he was rethinking his move to Charlotte in light of his father's return and his mother's refusal to go.

Skye wiped her fingers on a towel, gathered Romi and decided to talk Jake into staying—if not for him, then for his mother. If Jake left, his mother had no one, and she didn't deserve to spend her days alone without family around.

Rustic posts held up the small shed-like covering over the entrance to his building. Skye pressed the door open, and Jake looked up when she entered.

"The dresser is beautiful. I didn't get to tell you the last time I was in here."

He nodded. "I'm trying to get the top drawer to slide in smoother. A piece broke off the back and I repaired it, but something is still hanging the thing up and I can't figure out what."

Skye ran her fingers over the curved frame holding the mirror, keeping Romi's hand in hers so she didn't get hurt on any of the equipment in his shop. "I'm sure your mother will be happy when she sees the progress you've made."

"After tonight, the dresser may have to be my peace offering."

"I'm sure she'd like to see this dresser inside her home here. Not in Charlotte."

"What I don't understand is why she wants to see my father after everything he did to her."

"Maybe she's hoping to replace those bad memories from the past with good ones."

His phone vibrated on the shelf next to him. Jake paused tinkering on the drawer, reached for the device and placed the call on speaker. "Reed here."

"Hey, Jake." His father's voice filtered into the space. "I wanted to call and tell you Dante can meet with you tonight. He thinks he may have a lead on the identity of Lorna and Randy's killer. Can you meet at 7:00 p.m.?"

Skye watched turmoil deepen the lines on Jake's forehead. She couldn't imagine what he must be going through, having his father back in his life.

"He can't share the information over the phone?" Jake asked.

"He doesn't trust cell phones."

"Then I'll clean up and head to the hospital. Tell him to meet me in the lobby. Also, Mom wants to visit you."

A silent pause hung in the moment.

"Okay. Yeah, that's fine," his father said, his voice trembling through the speaker.

"Look, if you don't want her there, now is the time to say so. I'm not going to let you hurt her ever again. If you can't put on a smile and accommodate the woman who took the brunt of your sins, I'll make up a reason to cancel the visit."

Jake's face reddened from his neck into his cheeks. He'd always tried to look out for his mom, a trait Skye admired.

"I want to see her. I'm shocked she wants the same. Please, tell her I look forward to her visit."

"You better be nice, or you'll answer to me."

"I'm not the same man I used to be, Jake. I hope with time you'll see how God has changed me."

Skye hoped the man was sincere and not using God's name as a crutch to appease his family.

"I'm all about God changing people, Dad, but I'm going to need a bit more time before we welcome you back with open arms."

"Understood."

Jake ended the call, stood from his stool, and picked up the air hose, blowing the dust from his pants. "This might be over sooner than we thought. If Dante gives us a name, then I could make an arrest tonight."

Skye let Romi's hand go when the little girl moved to inspect the nozzle in Jake's hand he had used to clean up. He shot a burst of air at her tummy, and she giggled. "Again."

He repeated the gesture, and Romi laughed.

"Do you think Dante really knows the identity of Randy's—" Skye paused and motioned toward Romi, not wanting to say the word 'killer' in front of her daughter "—you know?"

"There's a good chance he does. Since we're both hunting for the same person, I don't think he would mislead us."

"You think he's on the up and up?"

"He's the only lead we have in regard to Lorna. If we find out what happened to her, then we solve Randy's case too."

Romi tugged on Jake's hand. "Again, Daddy."

Skye tensed at the word. She squatted next to her five-year-old. "Honey, this is Mr. Jake."

"I know, but I like to call him Daddy. Eli has

a daddy, too, but he's not here, either. We both decided to call Mr. Jake Daddy."

"Did you ask Mr. Jake if your new name was okay with him?"

"No." Big green eyes sure to melt any man's heart lifted to Jake. He shot a burst of air at Romi again. "You can call me anything you want, sweet girl. I don't mind."

"I guess she's been talking about her father with Eli. Thanks for understanding."

"Of course. Will you two be okay here while I'm gone? I'll make sure to have the guards on alert."

"We'll be fine. Bryn's coming over to give Romi a riding lesson. She called this morning. Someone told her about what happened, and she offered to give Romi several lessons for free in your new indoor riding arena. She probably wants to get her hooked so I'll have to pay for more lessons after all this blows over, but I thought it might be good for Romi to have something fun to do after the other night."

"Have her check in with the guards when she arrives, and they'll let her through."

"Great. Let me know what Dante says." She held out her hand to Romi. "We might be able to return to our house soon, little missy."

Romi's expression drooped. "I want to go back to Eli's and play with the barn animals."

Her daughter loved playing with her best

friend and chasing the goats or chickens across the yard. Skye breathed a thankful prayer her daughter remembered the good moments over the traumatic ones.

"We can come back and visit anytime you want, and I might even get a few chickens when we get home. Now, let's go get a snack before Ms. Bryn gets here for your pony ride."

Skye walked with her daughter as she skipped out the door. She glanced back over her shoulder at Jake and gave him a small wave. *He let Romi call him Daddy.*

Jake pushed down the sunshade in his truck and turned onto Hospital Drive. Nerves jittered through him at the thought of his mother visiting with his father. She kept wringing her hands while he drove. She must be feeling the nerves, too. She wore a blue blouse he hadn't seen on her in years. His father's favorite color. Jake wasn't sure about the meeting, but his mother had been adamant, especially after she found out he'd been sober for nine years.

Jake placed his hand on hers and gave them a squeeze.

"You look beautiful, Mom."

"Thanks, son. I'm a little nervous. Can you tell?"

"Only a little. Listen, I know Dad says he's changed, but I don't want you to get your hopes up too much, okay? Don't forget what he did to us."

"More of what he did to you." She pressed a soft hand to his cheek. "I'm so sorry—"

He covered her hand with his. "Mom, I'm fine. You don't have to apologize anymore. We've moved beyond regrets and sorrow, remember?"

"I guess some memories haunt us no matter how many times we receive forgiveness. If only I could go back."

"Well, we can't. We can move forward. Just be careful with your heart."

"I could say the same to you with Skye."

He pulled in front of the hospital entrance and stopped, hesitant to take his own advice. "I'll park the car. Why don't you wait in the lobby until I come up and we can go see him together?"

She reached for Jake's hand. "I need few minutes alone with your father."

"I don't think seeing him alone is a good idea."

"What did I say, Jake Reed? I'm a grown woman and can take care of myself. I'll be fine. I've toughened up in my old age, and I'll never let your father treat me or you the way he did before, but I need to do this. I need to look him in the eye and tell him things I should've said long ago but was too afraid. I'm not afraid anymore."

She opened the passenger door.

"I love you, Mom."

She turned back and faced him, her blue eyes

sparkling. She flashed a smile, lighting her entire countenance. No wonder his father fell for her. Even in her sixties, his mother was beautiful. "I love you, too, my sweet boy."

Jake watched her walk through the automatic doors opening to the interior of the building and prayed she found peace with her past and for her future.

Time was ticking, and Dante wasn't the kind of man to wait around for a meeting. Jake was headed toward the parking garage when his phone vibrated. Nate's name flashed across the screen. His partner had been investigating the financials of the warehouse bust.

They assumed Dante owned the building and if they followed the money trail to him, then Jake planned to arrest the man during the meeting instead of chatting with him. Of course, he'd wait to put the handcuffs on him after he found out the name of Randy's killer.

"Hey, man. Glad I caught you," Nate said.

"Tell me you got more evidence. I'm headed to meet with Dante at the hospital lobby in a few minutes. He told my father he had a new lead on our killer. Does he own the warehouse?"

"We traced the money through several shell corporations and found the owner, but it wasn't Carello."

"Then who owns the operation?"

"The warehouse belongs to Walter Cavanaugh."

"Bryn's husband? The horse guy?"

Cavanaugh had married into Bryn's family, whose wealth and influence permeated every organization in Crystal Creek. They had money spilling from their wallets.

Jake wound down the parking garage ramp. "They're filthy rich. Why would Walter be dealing?"

"Looks like he made several bad business investments and about a year ago, almost bankrupted the family business. He's been flushing money through the equestrian center ever since. We think he's laundering his drug money and trafficking fentanyl with the equestrian center as his front."

"And the money trail proves this?"

"Took me a while to trace the financials through all his back doors and ghost companies, but we've got him. His warehouses are set up all over the place. Kiam McClure was one of his runners, using the postal service delivery trucks to pick up the drugs from a couple of different warehouses and then transporting the product to Josephson Airfield. Walter owns the private strip, and from there he flies his product all over the nation."

"He must be the member Dante said went rogue, and Randy figured out what he did."

"There's more. Randy sent undercover detective, Hannah Barnes, into the equestrian center as a horse trainer. Her body was reported missing right before Randy was killed. We didn't put the two of them together because she died in a private plane crash."

"And they ruled her death an accident, too."

"Like Randy's."

Jake pulled into a parking space. "How does Lorna Daly fit into all of this? My father believes there's a connection to her death."

"I did a little digging on Lorna. She dumped Walter for Dante back when they were in college. But Walter wouldn't leave her alone. He harassed her and turned to threats. She took out a restraining order on Walter two weeks before he killed her. According to an anonymous tip, Walter lured Lorna to the top of Crystal Creek Falls by making her think she was meeting Dante there."

Jake decided to skip his meeting and pulled back onto the main road. "Do we have Walter in custody yet?"

"We sent officers to his home and business, but he wasn't there."

"Where is he?"

"We've got an APB out for him, but so far no one's spotted him or his truck."

Skye.

"Nate, get officers to my farmhouse. Bryn knows we moved Skye to the farm. She was coming over to give Romi riding lessons. If Walter knows their location, he'll target them there."

Jake ended the call and tapped Skye's number. The phone rang multiple times, then went to voice mail.

Walter Cavanaugh had killed his best friend. The man had looked him straight in the eye and lied when they questioned him at the equestrian center.

Jake flipped on his blue lights and siren, then called Dante to reschedule. The man confirmed his suspicions of Walter also.

He was only thirty minutes from Skye, but the drive seemed longer. She needed him more now than ever, and he had no way to warn her. No way to keep his promise to Randy.

Keep her safe, God. If You do, I'll never interfere in her life again.

NINETEEN

Skye let Romi skip ahead to the private arena on Jake's land, wearing her plaid cowgirl shirt and leather riding boots. She scrolled through the photos taken on her phone, smiling at her daughter's cute personality in each shot.

Bryn pulled her Chevy truck into the drive of the arena and slid from the driver's seat, then scooped Romi into her arms and kicked the truck door closed with her booted foot. "Hey, little lady. Are you ready to ride a miniature horse?"

"Yes, please."

Skye caught up to them. "Thanks so much for doing this, Bryn. She's been a little clingy since the other night. I can't even get her to go near the creek right now. She used to love playing in the water."

"I'm sure she'll get past the fear, right, Romster?" Skye's friend gave the little girl a bounce then slid her feet to the ground.

"Nope," Romi said.

Skye moved around to the horse trailer and helped Bryn open the doors.

"I brought Coco, your favorite horse from the center. Do you want to ride Coco?"

"Nope."

Skye squatted to her daughter's level. "Romi, Ms. Bryn came a long way to let you ride the horse, and you told me earlier you wanted to ride Coco. What's going on with you?"

"I'm scared, Mommy."

She wrapped her arms around her daughter. "Don't worry, sweet girl. I'll be right here with you the whole time. I won't let anything happen to you."

Bryn climbed into the trailer and backed the horse out, holding tight to the reins. "Coco is happy to see you, Romi, and I brought some apple pieces you can feed her."

Romi clung to Skye, not even wanting to pet the horse.

"I'm sure she'll be fine once we get inside the arena."

"Looks like the other night really did scare her."

Skye walked with Bryn into the building and closed the door once they were all inside. Her phone vibrated again in her pocket, but she ignored the call, wanting to focus on her daughter's needs. Bryn brought Coco close. Romi reached her hand out and petted the horse's nose.

"It scared all of us. I'm still having nightmares about the incident," Skye said.

"I can't even imagine what I would've done when the rope broke and she fell into the river. At least Jake had her."

"Momma, he's small like me."

Romi petted Coco's nose, and Skye contemplated Bryn's words. "Wait, how'd you know the rope broke?"

With a slight hesitation, Bryn flashed a smile. "I called Penny to check on you the other day, and she told me."

"But I never told Penny about the rope. In fact, I haven't had time to even call Penny since that night."

"Well, she must've heard the news from someone, because she told me."

"Word travels so fast in this town." Skye bent down in front of Romi. "Are you ready for Ms. Bryn to teach you more about riding the horse?"

Romi wrapped her arms around Skye's neck again and pulled her close. "You're staying, right?"

"Of course. I wouldn't miss seeing you ride for the world. You're going to do such a good job, and I'm going to get it on video so we can watch it over and over tonight."

Romi hugged her mom, then let go and stepped over to Coco. "Okay, Ms. Bryn. I'm ready now."

A loud clang echoed through the arena, and a side door opened, letting in a ray of bright light. The shadow of a large man stalked inside and pulled the door closed, engaging the slide lock at the top. Skye reached for Romi, but Bryn snatched the little girl into her arms and faced her friend, backing toward the door. "I'm so sorry to do this to you, Skye, but I'll do anything for my family."

Confused, Skye bounced her gaze between Bryn and the man. "What's going on? I don't understand."

He stalked toward them and pushed his cowboy hat back a bit, and the light reached his face. Walter joined his wife—a Glock in the holster, a skull tattoo on his forearm and a black-and-gold championship ring on his hand.

Romi cried and reached for her. "Don't let him take me again, Mommy."

Skye lunged for her daughter. Walter raised his behemoth arm, stopping her, and drummed his free fingertips across his gun. "I would stay where you are. You wouldn't want Romi to get hurt, would you?"

Memories from Randy's death poured through her mind like an ocean wave. She remembered his voice and the woman with him, seated on the passenger side of the truck.

"You killed Randy." She struggled to breathe.

"And Bryn, you were there. I remember now. You witnessed the whole thing and let me believe a lie for more than a year."

They were her friends, had brought her meals and comforted her after Randy's death. It was probably all a ploy to discover how much she knew about his murder.

Walter's strong grip squeezed her upper arm, causing the nerves in her fingers to tingle. He pressed the barrel of his gun into her side. "If you do everything I tell you, then Romi will have an amazing life. Bryn and I will take good care of her."

"I'm her mother. Romi needs to be with me."

"That's no longer an option, but I don't want to talk about this in front of our little girl. Bryn, take her out."

Romi cried and reached for her mother. Skye fought against him, but he overpowered her efforts. "You give my daughter to me and I promise not to hurt you or your family, Walter." Skye took two strides toward Bryn, but Walter's arm wrapped around her throat.

He nodded toward his wife. "Get the girl out of here." Bryn backed away toward the side door as Romi's cries intensified.

"Bryn, I'm warning you. Don't take my daughter." Skye struggled to free herself, but his grip tightened.

"Let's take a walk." His moist breath smelled of garlic and alcohol. He pulled her backward in the opposite direction, but she kept her gaze on Romi. Bryn opened the door and removed her daughter from the premises.

The side door slammed closed, the vibration thundering through Skye and into her soul. If she surrendered to him, he would kill her. She'd never be able to fight him off. His stature and strength overwhelmed most men in his presence, the same as on the night he towered over Randy and stabbed him in the side of his neck.

Walter shoved her toward another side door on the opposite side of the arena. She didn't fight back. Not yet.

They walked for what seemed like miles on a path behind Jake's property, into the thick wooded area above Crystal Creek. Brush and thorns snagged Skye's jeans, and the uphill stride made her calf muscles ache. Water swirled below, and white rapids churned into dangerous currents no one should cross. Trees thinned as they neared the pinnacle.

At the end of the trail was an eighty-foot drop into a raging lagoon, waiting to swallow those who slipped from the mountain heights. A six-foot chain link fence had been erected along the trail three years ago, after several hikers fell to their deaths.

"This is how you killed Lorna. She didn't fall. You pushed her."

He shoved the gun into her back. "Keep walking."

"What happened, Walter? Did Lorna realize what kind of evil heart you had and decide she wanted nothing to do with you?"

He exhaled a sinister chuckle. "Lorna didn't know a good thing when she had it. She tramped off to be with Dante Carello, but I took care of her. I would've gotten him, too, but he ganged up and built an army to protect himself. I'm still working on a plan for him."

Skye looked for anything to use as a weapon. Only mountain laurels and thick underbrush filled the edges of the path.

The trees of the forest cleared, and thunderous rapids roared nearby. Dirt underneath Skye's shoes turned to rock, and the brush parted. Walter reached for a severed breach in the chain link fence, lifted the corner and created an opening large enough to crawl through.

"Go on," he said and motioned with his gun.

Skye stepped to the other side and stood at the top of Crystal Creek Falls, trying not to look down. Instead, she focused her gaze on Walter who followed her. "You've become an expert at making death look like an accident, haven't you?"

"Kind of my specialty."

"And Bryn, does she know what you do in your spare time?"

"My wife trusts I'll take care of her and our business. She learned a long time ago not to ask questions and decided to be happy with her horses and money. I tend to keep the dirtier sides of the business to myself."

"By murdering innocent people?"

"You lived a quiet life with Romi and all was good until you talked your boyfriend into re-opening Randy's case."

"Jake isn't my boyfriend, and Randy was one of the best men out there. His heart was good and kind, unlike yours."

Walter shoved her closer to the edge. She had to buy some time, not for herself but for her daughter. By the time Jake talked to Dante and discovered Walter's identity, he might have time to rescue Romi, but Skye's life was sure to end here.

Carli had agreed a long time ago to care for Romi should anything happen to Skye. Her sweet little girl would grow up with Eli on the ranch petting the farm animals every day.

But she wasn't dead yet, and she searched the ground for anything to help her escape.

Walter stepped toward her, gun still in hand. Warm wind whipped around them.

Draw him closer to the edge.

She stepped to the side a bit. Uneven surfaces

tripped up many hikers who plunged to their death off cliffs, and she wanted to make sure she had solid footing on the rock.

"Move on over to the edge." He waved the end of the gun in the direction he wanted her to go.

Skye took one step closer, leaving about five feet from the rim. "I remember Lorna. She was a sweet girl who was never outdoorsy. She liked books, studying and was well on her way to being valedictorian. Her favorite spot was the Crystal Creek Library. I remember because I used to see her there all the time when we were teenagers. She tutored you. Helped you get your grades up so you could stay on the football team. Yet this is how you repaid her." Skye reached for her phone, still in her back pocket.

"She slipped."

"Is that what you're going to tell the cops when they recover my body from the bottom of the river?"

"Bryn and I'll be long gone by then. Now, turn around and take a step closer."

Skye pulled her cell and turned her body in one swift motion. Walter didn't notice the phone in her hand.

With her thumb on the side button ready to hit three quick strikes and activate the SOS feature, her only hope was Jake would receive the photo of Walter and her location in time. She squeezed her eyes closed, rotated back to face her killer and held up her phone.

"Smile for the camera."

Her thumb hit the key three times in succession. Walter charged toward her with the gun pointed at her head. This was it—if she didn't fight, provide DNA under her nails or something, they would think she fell to her death. The odds were against her.

God help me.

He grabbed her arm pulling her toward the edge. Skye reached over and clawed his face, making sure to dig deep into his skin.

"Stupid broad."

His free hand flew to the cut, wiped the blood, then landed a strike against her cheek.

Speckles dotted her vision, and an instant burn radiated into her eye. His strength overpowered her. Skye clung to him and pushed her thumbs into his eye sockets, but he broke her hold and flung her body away from him.

She landed and rolled, grasping for any hold to stop the momentum. With a final grip on the edge of a rock, her body lunged over the side. Sharp edges cut into the palms of her hands, but she didn't let go. Water from the falls sprayed against her side, creating a slippery foothold.

Walter stepped to the edge, the shadow of his body looming over her. "Let go and you can be with Randy again."

Skye's arms burned as her strength faded. Her feet scratched at the rock's vertical surface, trying to find any notch to provide some stability.

"Walter. Don't move and drop your weapon." Jake's voice drifted to her.

The man's lips curved into a smile. His finger slid to the trigger, and he turned his back on Skye.

"Jake!" The roar of the waterfall swallowed her cry. She struggled to grip the edge of the rock.

"Step away from the edge and place your gun on the ground," Jake said again.

Walter stood, unmoving.

"On your knees, now. Skye, hang tight. I'm coming."

Walter didn't budge.

Her strength faded, and her fingers slipped. "Jake."

Skye dug her toes onto a thin ledge and pushed up. Her weight lifted. She pulled enough to get her forearms resting on the rock's surface and crawled back on the ledge.

Jake kept Walter distracted. "You're under arrest, Walter, and I'm going to personally make sure you go to jail for a very long time."

"For what?"

"For the murders of Lorna Daly, Randy Anderson and Kiam McClure."

Walter stepped toward Jake. "What about Skye Anderson? Are you going to add her to the list?"

She seized the moment and with a reach to her left, Skye gripped an ample-size rock and rose to her feet. She swung and connected with the back of Walter's head.

The man spun around and lunged for her again. Shots fired. She ducked, placing a shoulder into Walter's torso, then lifted with all the strength she could muster. His massive frame toppled off balance and propelled him forward.

He clawed at the air, reaching for a hold, but missed. A deep guttural scream met her ears, and he disappeared over the edge.

Nothing but the roar of the waterfalls followed.

Skye stood frozen for a moment then inched her way to the periphery. She stared into the water below. Walter, the man who had murdered her husband, sank into the depths of Crystal Creek.

Jake rushed to her and pulled her into his arms. "Are you okay?"

She stepped back and moved toward the trail. There was no time to waste ruminating over what she'd done. "Bryn has Romi, and I've got to stop her."

"Nate and several other officers stopped Bryn's truck and trailer near the county line and found Romi inside. Nate's bringing your daughter back to the ranch and will stay with her until you get there."

Skye jumped into his arms again. "Thank you for looking out for us. How'd you know?"

"We traced the financials of the warehouse and Josephson Airfield back to Walter and Bryn. They've been using the equestrian center as a cover for his operation. She turned on Walter and told us everything."

Jake glanced over the edge to the bottom of the river. Officers stationed across the banks below retrieved Walter's body. He was dead.

"He tried to kill you. He didn't want you to remember his presence at Randy's crime scene. He came at you full force, ready to shove you over the edge. If you hadn't ducked, I'm not sure you'd be standing here right now."

Skye's body trembled against his. "He killed Lorna and Randy. He made their deaths look like accidents and would've gotten away with the murders had you not reopened the case."

"There may be more. We'll look back at any accidents from the time of Lorna's death and Randy's. If he was hiding his true operation, then there's no telling how many people he killed." Jake gave Skye a squeeze. "You're safe now."

"What about Carello?"

"There's no ties between them, except for Walter recruiting a couple of his low-level thugs on the side. He doesn't work for Carello. In fact,

Carello was in love with Lorna and wanted her killer brought to justice. You and Romi are safe now and can go home."

Her lips curved into a slow smile. "I've wanted to hear you say those words for so long."

"I'll try not to take offense to your enthusiasm in moving out of my house."

"And I can go back to work?"

"You can. Penny's been cleared of all charges, and your postmaster has put in new guidelines to keep all the drivers accountable."

Skye leaned into his arms again. "That's so great. Romi and I can return to our normal lives."

He hugged her a little tighter and a little longer, caressing the ends of her hair. He didn't want to let her go, but he might as well let this moment be goodbye. She didn't need him to protect her anymore.

"Wait, what about you? You're staying in Crystal Creek, right?"

Jake released her. "Sergeant Butler wants me in Charlotte as soon as possible. We made things easier for Carello to expand his drug ring into Walter's now-vacant territory. The money he 'encouraged' business owners to give to his charity for inner-city kids went to expand his operation. The task force I'll be running will attack the entire network Carello operates."

"I see. When do you leave?"

"In two days."

She gave him a small nod, then leaned toward him, placing her lips to his cheek. "If you ever change your mind and decide to come home, I'll be here."

Without another word, Skye moved back toward the path and disappeared out of sight. Jake turned and inhaled a deep breath and stared out across the Blue Ridge Mountains. He'd left once and regretted his decision, but if he stayed, he faced something much more intimidating than any killer…marriage.

TWENTY

Jake found his mom standing at the kitchen window while she scrubbed a plate, her gaze focused outside. She wiped her hands on a towel and faced him when he shuffled into the space. "This house is going to be awful lonely without you, Skye and Romi here anymore."

"I told you, I'll come up from Charlotte and spend every weekend with you. Plus, Skye promised to come by every day and help with your medicine. She doesn't live far from here, so if you need anything, give her a call."

His mother placed the dish into the plastic drain next to her sink. "Why can't you stay? You don't need to take the job in Charlotte when you have a great place to work right here in Crystal Creek. Besides, you never liked living in the big city. The first time you were there, you complained about the traffic and nosy neighbors if I recall correctly."

She had a point. Almost one million people

called Charlotte, North Carolina, home and even though it was only two hours away from Crystal Creek, the two places were like different worlds.

Traffic here never backed up unless one of the farmers drove his tractor down Main Street. In Charlotte, Jake fought traffic every day.

But his expertise on Dante Carello and the cartel the man operated made Jake an expert and ideal for overseeing the task force.

After news spread of Walter's death, Dante wasted no time snatching up the vacant drug territory. If the man gained any more ground, his fame, power and notoriety would surpass the worst drug lords in history. Jake's expertise could stop him, even if he had to leave his mother in Crystal Creek for now.

He took his mom's hand. "Come with me. I want to show you something."

He laced her hand through his arm and escorted her out the side door and into his wood shop. Jake stepped to the side and flipped on his light. In the middle of the room sat the finished dresser his mother loved. Her eyes grew wide with tears, and she stepped closer.

"You finished the dresser. It's beautiful."

Her hand traced the curved pieces holding the antique mirror and then pulled him into a hug. "I can't believe you were able to fix something so broken."

He smiled and hugged her back. "You deserve it, Mom. I can move the piece into the house tonight, if you show me the location you prefer."

His mother placed a hand on his face. "You're such a good man, Jake Reed. I don't know if I tell you enough, but you are. You deserve amazing things in your life, too."

Her words resonated, breaking emotions inside him. He fought back the unfamiliar sting of tears, not wanting to cry in front of his mother, but her affirmation spoke love right into the dark wounds his father had created a long time ago.

She took his hand, led him out the door and stood underneath the covered awning of his shop, then pointed toward the tire swing. Romi squealed with delight as Skye pushed her daughter a little higher.

"See those two people, right over there? God put them on this earth for you. They're what a good Father gives to His faithful son, even when he's too stubborn to see love right in front of his eyes."

"Mom, I don't think—"

She held up a hand. "I know love, son, and that woman loves you. I also know you." She placed her hand on his chest. "…and you love her. It's time to let go of the past, of your father and even of me. Take the dresser you restored and start something fresh and new with Skye."

Jake stared at the beautiful woman swinging with her daughter, the woman his heart longed to love more than anyone else. "What if I mess up like Dad did?"

"Oh, I can guarantee you'll mess up, but you're not your father, Jake. You know the pain he caused, how the scars linger, and your heart will never do the same to someone you love. Trust yourself for once. Trust Skye. But most of all, trust God."

His mother patted his arm and left him standing in the doorway with a straight-line view of his potential future. God never promised life would be easy. In fact, Jake had suffered more bad than good. But through all the abuse and conflict, God always provided a way out and never left him alone. God's goodness surrounded him now. Love was right in front of him. All he had to do was accept the gift.

Skye lifted her suitcases from Jake's SUV and sat them on the front porch of her home. She inhaled the honeysuckled air around her and noted the weeds overgrown in her flower garden. For once, she didn't mind thinking about the work her yard needed.

Jake closed the hatch and laughed at Romi, who led Sully around outside on his leash, like a horse with a bridle. Several times, Skye pulled her daughter from the dog's back, reminding Romi Sully wasn't a horse and he liked to be scratched, not ridden.

"How does it feel to be home again?" Jake asked, joining her on the porch.

"Good. Thank you for letting us stay with you. I'm not sure what we would've done had you not returned to Crystal Creek."

"Probably never moved in the first place."

"I doubt that. Once I told Bryn about my memories, Walter was bound to come for me, but you kept us safe."

"Zain brought charges against Bryn for kidnapping Romi and her involvement with Walter's nefarious business dealings. She'll be in prison for a long time."

The conversation faded, but Skye didn't want their time together to end. Tomorrow, Jake would leave. First thing in the morning, he would start his new job two hours away.

Without Randy here, who was going to pick up the broken pieces of her heart this time? Her chest tightened with the thought, and she fought the bitter sting of regret.

"How's your father doing?"

"He was discharged to the rehab facility until he gets stronger."

"And your mom? Is she okay with him being back in town?"

A smile curled on his lips—the same lips she hoped would kiss her goodbye. "My mom visited him in the hospital and apparently told him how things were going to be if he was here to stay. She's made peace with their past, and he has jumped to accommodate everything she's requested."

"Do you think they'll get back together?"

Jake shook his head. "I don't think so. He did so much damage, but Mom's helping him with his rehab. You should see her when he starts to complain. She cracks the whip and makes him work harder."

"And you? Have you come to terms with his return?"

"To be honest, I'm still struggling with him being back. I even talked to the doctor about sending him to another city to get rehab, but he refused, saying he needed to keep an eye on my father's progress. Then the man gave me the number for Dad's therapist and told me to call him."

"What for?"

"Since I'm listed as Dad's medical power of attorney, the therapist shared my father's journey to wellness. He's been through a lot in the last nine years, but with work, he overcame his addiction and now mentors other alcoholics. He hasn't had any violent episodes since he quit drinking, so I'm willing to give him a cautious chance, but I'll be keeping my guard up for a while."

Skye stepped close to him. "I'm so thankful you've been able to work through some of those things. Don't worry. I'll keep an eye on your mom and let you know if anything seems out of balance—unless I can change your mind about going to Charlotte."

Skye understood the importance of his position but hoped they could work out some kind of compromise. She'd fallen for Jake again and didn't want him to leave.

He held out his hand. "Can I show you something?"

"Sure." She slipped her fingers into his palm.

He opened the front door of her home, then led her inside, stopping in the center of the living space. "My mother wanted you to have this."

Jake stepped to the side and revealed the refurbished dresser.

Skye's hand pressed against her chest, then traced the grain of the wood smoothed by Jake's hands. "You finished the dresser. It's beautiful. But I can't keep this. The piece belongs to your mom."

"She said new beginnings deserve a new piece of furniture."

Skye circled the dresser, taking in every ornate detail. Attention and love dressed the outside, and three drawers, all the same size, filled the frame.

"May I see inside?" she asked.

Jake took hold of the knob and slid the top drawer open. Skye peeked into the velvet-lined space. A small blue box sat inside. Her name was written on a gold tag fastened through the hinge. She lifted the box and faced him.

"Is this for me?"

"Open it," he said.

Skye eased back the cover and gasped—an antique diamond ring rested within the slit cushion.

"This was my grandmother's ring." Jake took the jewelry from the box, lifted her left hand in his and kissed her fingers. "You captured my heart many years ago and I've always loved you Skye, even when we were apart. I know I've told you I wasn't ready to be a husband and father because of what I experienced as a child, but truth is, I want a family, more than anything. I want you and Romi to be my family, forever."

Skye swallowed, trying to absorb the change in his mind-set. "Does that mean you're staying in Crystal Creek?"

"I talked with the sergeant, and with a few trips to Charlotte, he said I can run the joint task force from here and he'll oversee the team there. Skye, I let you go once before, and I'm not leaving you again."

She pulled his lips to hers. Soft and longing,

years of pent-up desire and love deepened their kiss. His hand tightened against her back, pulling her closer, washing away any friction between them, their future smooth like the stones of Crystal Creek.

* * * * *

*If you liked this story from Shannon Redmon,
check out her previous
Love Inspired Suspense book,*
Cave of Secrets
Available now from Love Inspired Suspense!

*Find more great reads at
www.LoveInspired.com.*

Dear Reader,

Jake and Skye's story unveils God's forgiveness and their renewed love, set in the fictional town of Crystal Creek, North Carolina—modeled after a small town in the Blue Ridge Mountains.

Skye appeared in my first book, *Cave of Secrets*, as the postal supervisor. Many thanks to my cousin Carrie Pless, who answered all my questions about the tasks of a postal carrier. She brought authenticity to the story in both books.

Jake struggles with his past and becoming the man God wants him to be. Although I was raised in a supportive, loving home, many children are not, and I wanted to show God's grace and provision through the horrific times life can bring.

I love hearing from readers!

You can contact me through my website at www.shannonredmon.com, through Facebook at https://www.facebook.com/shannon.redmon or email me at shannon@shannonredmon.com.

Blessings and love,
Shannon Redmon